The yellowbacks... classics of popular fiction

The yellowjackets or yellowbacks were a great series of bestselling adventure and crime thrillers that had its origins in the mid to late 19th century following on from the 'penny dreadfuls'. They virtually began the mass market revolution of the early 20th century with a clear standard format and imprint/series livery (what would today be called branding). Hodder & Stoughton published the yellowjackets in two main series with series run dates of: 1923-1939 and later 1949-1957.

As the tagline ('where thrillers really began') on the back cover implies, the imprint and series focused on thrillers that were the bestsellers of their time. This current reissue or retro revival if you will, brings back many of these masterpieces, now classics in their own way and extends it further by including key titles from that period that were either great crime or thriller or even general commercial fiction (including sub-genres of noir, horror, gothic, romance, westerns, etc.) influences of their time. There are some perennial favourites and many rarities either lost or not easily available being revived in the current series. Writers and characters ranged from adventure heroes like Bulldog Drummond, Allan Quatermain, Richard Hannay or the Saint through thriller grandmasters Edgar Wallace and E. Phillips Oppenheim, crime and mystery maestros like Patricia Wentworth, G.K. Chesterton, Agatha Christie and the Detection club, to western and swashbucklers like Zane Grey, Max Brand, Captain Blood and even romance or general fiction classics like Hermina Black, Denise Robins, Marie Corelli or Stella Morton. These were books that had storytelling at their heart and always entertained.

The yellowbacks had both hardback (with varying design elements) and paperback (which built the series look) versions with the latter still carrying the imprint 'yellowjacket'. The current reissues pay tribute to both and use an amalgam of elements from both editions while retaining the complete yellow (or 'mustard-plaster') livery with the author's name in blue beveled type with a 'simulated emboss' effect and a white outer 'outline', and the book title in black. These reissues retain the distinctive size of the original mass market paperback and follow the three main category variations—the thrillers (crime, westerns, mystery, adventure) had blue lettering for the author's name, while Romance and softer general fiction had red; and other categories like humour had green.

For more details and a full list of titles visit https://www.hachetteindia.com/home/yellowbacks

MARY LOUISE

MARY LOUISE

Frank L. Baum (May 15, 1856 – May 6, 1919) is one of America's most read authors, and he is widely considered one of the premier authors of children's books. Baum wrote dozens of novels and short stories, as well as hundreds of poems, and he even foresaw technological innovations such as computers, televisions and mobile phones, all of which made their way into his writing.

Although Frank L. Baum is best remembered as the author of the Wizard of Oz series of books, he also penned a variety of stories geared for young readers under various pen names. Mary Louise is part of Baum's Bluebird Books series, which centres on the exploits and triumphs of intrepid teen detective Mary Louise Burrows. There were ten books in the series but interestingly though she was created that way on the publisher's behest, Mary Louise proved "too tame" a character to drive the series forward and the less traditional Josie O'Gorman, girl agent, came to dominate more and more; and by the last three books had taken over the series.

MARY LOUISE

L. Frank Baum

Mary Louise
First published by Reilly & Britton in 1916.

This Hodder Yellowback edition © Hachette India 2023
(Registered Name: Hachette Book Publishing India Pvt. Ltd.)
An Hachette UK Company www.hachetteindia.com

1

All rights reserved. No part of the publication may be reproduced, stored in a retrieval system (including but not limited to computers, disks, external drives, electronic or digital devices, e-readers, websites), or transmitted in any form or by any means (including but not limited to cyclostyling, photocopying, docutech or other reprographic reproductions, mechanical, recording, electronic, digital versions) without the prior written permission of the publisher, nor be otherwise circulated in any form of binding or cover other than that in which it is published and without a similar condition being imposed on the subsequent purchaser.

The texts in these editions in most cases have been reprinted as is, with minimal editorial changes and by and large no bowdlerizing for political correctness; though in some editions, a few words and phrases considered archaic, or those considered offensive now, along with archaic punctuation may have been modified in places to make the text more accessible to today's readers. The narratives, language, beliefs, social mores and/or cultural depictions, in these volumes are a reflection of their times and must be viewed as such. They may also contain certain cultural, racial and gender prejudices and stereotypes that may be outdated or clearly wrong then and wrong today; but their removal would be tantamount to claiming these prejudices never existed. The Publisher does not endorse or support those depictions or stereotypes; and these books have been made available for a discerning audience that will read it for entertainment value and a chronicle/record of popular fiction of past times.

Cover design by Priya Singh adapted from the original classic yellowjacket by Hodder & Stoughton.

Cover illustration by Ishan Trivedi.

Series note: Some of the books in the series (unless otherwise credited) may have cover or inside illustrations from the original yellowbacks or early editions, and while full restoration has been attempted, some images may be grainy or faded due to the condition of the original material. The end notes or bonus material or blurb details may have been sourced from the public domain or free use publications such as Wikipedia and attribution is hereby made also allowing similar free use reproduction from here. Sources requiring further specific attribution may write in and further detailing and/or corrections shall be made in subsequent printings/editions.

Reprint specifications may be subject to change including but not limited to finishes, paper, colour sections.

ISBN: 978-93-5731-150-2

Hachette Book Publishing India Pvt. Ltd.
4th & 5th Floors, Corporate Centre,
Plot No. 94, Sector 44, Gurugram - 122 003, India

Typeset in Electra LT STD 10/12.5 pt by Manipal Technologies Limited, Manipal

Printed and bound in India by Manipal Technologies Limited, Manipal

CONTENTS

I.	Just An Argument	1
II.	Gran'pa Jim	6
III.	A Surprise	12
IV.	Shifting Sands	17
V.	Official Investigation	21
VI.	Under A Cloud	29
VII.	The Escape	36
VIII.	A Friendly Foe	42
IX.	Officer O'gorman	50
X.	Rather Queer Indeed	59
XI.	Mary Louise Meets Irene	64
XII.	A Cheerful Comrade	73
XIII.	Bub Succumbs To Force	78
XIV.	A Call From Agatha Lord	87
XV.	Bub's Hobby	95
XVI.	The Stolen Book	102
XVII.	The Hired Girl	105
XVIII.	Mary Louise Grows Suspicious	110
XIX.	An Artful Confession	116

XX.	Diamond Cut Diamond	124
XXI.	Bad News	134
XXII.	The Folks At Bigbee's	138
XXIII.	A Kiss From Josie	144
XXIV.	Facing The Truth	149
XXV.	Simple Justice	155
XXVI.	The Letter	160

I

JUST AN ARGUMENT

"It's positively cruel!" pouted Jennie Allen, one of a group of girls occupying a garden bench in the ample grounds of Miss Stearne's School for Girls, at Beverly.

"It's worse than that; it's insulting," declared Mable Westervelt, her big dark eyes flashing indignantly.

"Doesn't it seem to reflect on our characters?" timidly asked Dorothy Knerr.

"Indeed it does!" asserted Sue Finley. "But here comes Mary Louise; let's ask her opinion."

"Phoo! Mary Louise is only a day scholar," said Jennie. "The restriction doesn't apply to her at all."

"I'd like to hear what she says, anyhow," remarked Dorothy. "Mary Louise has a way of untangling things, you know."

"She's rather too officious to suit me," Mable Westervelt retorted, "and she's younger than any of us. One would think, the way she poses as monitor at this second-rate, run-down boarding school, that Mary Louise Burrows made the world."

"Oh, Mable! I've never known her to pose at all," said Sue. "But, hush; she mustn't overhear us and, besides, if we want her to intercede with Miss Stearne we must not offend her."

The girl they were discussing came leisurely down a path, her books under one arm, the other hand holding a class paper which she examined in a cursory way as she walked. She wore a dark skirt and a simple shirtwaist, both quite modish and becoming, and her shoes were the admiration and envy of half the girls at the school. Dorothy Knerr used to say that "Mary Louise's clothes always looked as if they grew on her," but that may have been partially accounted for by the grace of her slim form and her unconscious but distinctive poise of bearing. Few people would describe Mary Louise Burrows as beautiful, while all would agree that she possessed charming manners. And she was fifteen — an age when many girls are both awkward and shy.

As she drew near to the group on the bench they ceased discussing Mary Louise but continued angrily to canvass their latest grievance.

"What do you think, Mary Louise," demanded Jennie, as the girl paused before them, "of this latest outrage?"

"What outrage, Jen?" with a whimsical smile at their indignant faces.

"This latest decree of the tyrant Stearne. Didn't you see it posted on the blackboard this morning? 'The young ladies will hereafter refrain from leaving the school grounds after the hour of six p.m., unless written permission is first secured from the Principal. Any infraction of this rule will result in suspension or permanent dismissal.' We're determined not to stand for this rule a single minute. We intend to strike for our liberties."

"Well," said Mary Louise reflectively, "I'm not surprised. The wonder is that Miss Stearne hasn't stopped your evening parades before now. This is a small school in a small town, where everyone knows everyone else; otherwise you'd have been guarded as jealously as if you were in a convent. Did you ever know or hear of any other private boarding school where the girls were allowed to go to town evenings, or whenever they pleased out of school hours?"

JUST AN ARGUMENT

"Didn't I tell you?" snapped Mable, addressing the group. "Mary Louise is always on the wrong side. Other schools are not criterions for this ramshackle establishment, anyhow. We have twelve boarders and four day scholars, and how Miss Stearne ever supports the place and herself on her income is an occult problem that the geometries can't solve. She pays little Miss Dandler, her assistant, the wages of an ordinary housemaid; the furniture is old and shabby and the classrooms gloomy; the food is more nourishing than feastful and the tablecloths are so patched and darned that it's a wonder they hold together."

Mary Louise quietly seated herself upon the bench beside them.

"You're looking on the seamy side, Mable," she said with a smile, "and you're not quite just to the school. I believe your parents sent you here because Miss Stearne is known to be a very competent teacher and her school has an excellent reputation of long standing. For twenty years this delightful old place, which was once General Barlow's residence, has been a select school for young ladies of the best families. Gran'pa Jim says it's an evidence of good breeding and respectability to have attended Miss Stearne's school."

"Well, what's that got to do with this insulting order to stay in evenings?" demanded Sue Finley. "You'd better put all that rot you're talking into a circular and mail it to the mothers of imbecile daughters. Miss Stearne has gone a step too far in her tyranny, as she'll find out. We know well enough what it means. There's no inducement for us to wander into that little tucked-up town of Beverly after dinner except to take in the picture show, which is our one innocent recreation. I'm sure we've always conducted ourselves most properly. This order simply means we must cut out the picture show and, if we permit it to stand, heaven only knows what we shall do to amuse ourselves."

"We'll do something worse, probably," suggested Jennie.

"What's your idea about it, Mary Louise?" asked Dorothy.

"Don't be a prude," warned Mable, glaring at the young girl. "Try to be honest and sensible—if you can—and give us your advice. Shall we disregard the order, and do as we please, or be namby-pambies and submit to the outrage? You're a day scholar and may visit the picture shows as often as you like. Consider our position, cooped up here like a lot of chickens and refused the only harmless amusement the town affords."

"Gran'pa Jim," observed Mary Louise, musingly, "always advises me to look on both sides of a question before making up my mind, because every question has to have two sides or it couldn't be argued. If Miss Stearne wishes to keep you away from the pictures, she has a reason for it; so let's discover what the reason is."

"To spoil any little fun we might have," asserted Mable bitterly.

"No; I can't believe that," answered Mary Louise. "She isn't unkindly, we all know, nor is she too strict with her girls. I've heard her remark that all her boarders are young ladies who can be trusted to conduct themselves properly on all occasions; and she's right about that. We must look for her reason somewhere else and I think it's in the pictures themselves."

"As for that," said Jennie, "I've seen Miss Stearne herself at the picture theatre twice within the last week."

"Then that's it; she doesn't like the character of the pictures shown. I think, myself, girls, they've been rather rank lately."

"What's wrong with them?"

"I like pictures as well as you do," said Mary Louise, "and Gran'pa Jim often takes me to see them. Tuesday night a man shot another in cold blood and the girl the murderer was in love with helped him to escape and married him. I felt like giving her a good shaking, didn't you? She didn't act like a real girl at all. And Thursday night the picture story told of a man with two wives and of divorces and disgraceful doings generally. Gran'pa Jim took me away before it was over and

I was glad to go. Some of the pictures are fine and dandy, but as long as the man who runs the theatre mixes the horrid things with the decent ones—and we can't know beforehand which is which—it's really the safest plan to keep away from the place altogether. I'm sure that's the position Miss Stearne takes, and we can't blame her for it. If we do, it's an evidence of laxness of morals in ourselves."

The girls received this statement sullenly, yet they had no logical reply to controvert it. So Mary Louise, feeling that her explanation of the distasteful edict was not popular with her friends, quietly rose and sauntered to the gate, on her way home.

"Pah!" sneered Mable Westervelt, looking after the slim figure, "I'm always suspicious of those goody-goody creatures. Mark my words, girls: Mary Louise will fall from her pedestal some day. She isn't a bit better than the rest of us, in spite of her angel baby ways, and I wouldn't be surprised if she turned out to be a regular hypocrite!"

II

GRAN'PA JIM

Beverly is an old town and not especially progressive. It lies nearly two miles from a railway station and has little attractiveness for strangers. Beverly contains several beautiful old residences, however, built generations ago and still surrounded by extensive grounds where the trees and shrubbery are now generally overgrown and neglected.

One of these fine old places Miss Stearne rented for her boarding school; another, quite the most imposing residence in the town, had been leased some two years previous to the time of this story by Colonel James Weatherby, whose family consisted of his widowed daughter, Mrs Burrows, and his grandchild, Mary Louise Burrows. Their only servants were an old black man, Uncle Eben, and his wife, Aunt Polly, who were Beverly bred and had been hired when the Colonel first came to town and took possession of the stately Vandeventer mansion.

Colonel Weatherby was a man of exceptionally distinguished appearance, tall and dignified, with courtly manners and an air of prosperity that impressed the simple villagers with awe. His snow-white hair and piercing dark eyes, his immaculate dress upon all occasions, the whispered comments on his ample deposits in the local bank, all contributed to render him remarkable among the three or four hundred ordinary inhabitants of Beverly, who, after his two years' residence among them, scarcely knew more of him than is above related. For Colonel Weatherby was an extremely reserved man and seldom deigned to exchange conversation with his neighbors. In truth, he had nothing in common with them and even when he walked out with Mary Louise he merely acknowledged the greeting of those he met by a dignified nod of his stately head.

With Mary Louise, however, he would converse fluently and with earnestness, whether at home during the long evenings or on their frequent walks through the country, which were indulged in on Saturdays and holidays during the months that school was in session and much more often during vacations. The Colonel owned a modest automobile which he kept in the stable and only drove on rare occasions, although one of Uncle Eben's duties was to keep the car in apple-pie order. Colonel Weatherby loved best to walk and Mary Louise enjoyed their tramps together because Gran'pa Jim always told her so many interesting things and was such a charming companion. He often developed a strain of humor in the girl's society and would relate anecdotes that aroused in her spontaneous laughter, for she possessed a keen sense of the ludicrous. Yes, Gran'pa Jim was really funny, when in the mood, and as jolly a comrade as one would wish.

He was fond of poetry, too, and the most severe trial Mary Louise was forced to endure was when he carried a book of poems in his pocket and insisted on reading from it while they rested in a shady nook by the roadside or on the bank of the little river that flowed near by the town. Mary Louise had no soul for poetry, but she would have endured far greater hardships rather than forfeit the genial companionship of Gran'pa Jim.

It was only during these past two years that she had come to know her grandfather so intimately and to become as fond of him as she was proud. Her earlier life had been one of so many changes that the constant shifting had rather bewildered her. First she remembered living in a big city house where she was cared for by a nurse who was never out of sight or hearing. There it was that "Mamma Bee"—Mrs Beatrice Burrows—appeared to the child at times as a beautiful vision and often as she bent over her little daughter for a goodnight kiss the popular society woman, arrayed in evening or ball costume, would seem to Mary Louise like a radiant angel descended straight from heaven.

She knew little of her mother in those days, which were quite hazy in memory because she was so young. The first change she remembered was an abrupt flitting from the splendid city house to a humble cottage in a retired village. There was no maid now, nor other servant whatever. Mamma Bee did the cooking and sweeping, her face worn and anxious, while Gran'pa Jim walked the floor of the little sitting room day by day, only pausing at times to read to Mary Louise stories from her nursery books.

This life did not last very long—perhaps a year or so—and then they were in a big hotel in another city, reached after a long and tiresome railway journey. Here the girl saw little of her grandfather, for a governess came daily to teach Mary Louise to read and write and to do sums on a pretty slate framed in silver. Then, suddenly, in dead of night, away they whisked again, traveling by train until long after the sun was up, when they came to a pretty town where they kept house again.

There were servants, this time, and horses and carriages and pretty clothes for Mary Louise and Mamma Bee. The little girl was sent to a school just a block away from her home. She remembered Miss Jenkins well, for this teacher made much of her and was so kind and gentle that Mary Louise progressed rapidly in her studies.

But the abrupt changes did not end here. Mary Louise came home from school one afternoon and found her dear mother sobbing bitterly as she clung around the neck of Gran'pa Jim, who stood in the middle of the room as still as if he had been a marble statue. Mary Louise promptly mingled her tears with those of her mother, without knowing why, and then there was a quick "packing-up" and a rush to the railway again.

Next they were in the house of Mr and Mrs Peter Conant, very pleasant people who seemed to be old friends of Mamma Bee and Gran'pa Jim. It was a cosy house, not big and pretentious, and Mary Louise liked it. Peter Conant and Gran'pa Jim had many long talks together, and it was here that the child first heard her grandfather called "Colonel." Others might have called him that before, but she had not heard them. Mrs Conant was very deaf and wore big spectacles, but she always had a smile on her face and her voice was soft and pleasing.

After a few days Mamma Bee told her daughter she was going to leave her in the care of the Conants for a time, while she traveled to a foreign country with Gran'pa Jim. The girl was surprised at being abandoned but accepted her fate quietly when it was explained that she was to go to school while living with the Conants, which she could not do if she was traveling with her mother and grandfather, who were making this arrangement for the girl's best good.

Three years Mary Louise lived with the Conants and had little to complain of. Mr Conant was a lawyer and was at his office all day, while Mrs Conant was very kind to the girl and looked after her welfare with motherly care.

At last, quite unexpectedly, Mary Louise's trunk was packed and she was taken to the station to meet a train on which were her mother and grandfather. They did not leave the cars except to shake hands with the Conants and thank them for their care of Mary Louise. A moment later the train bore away the reunited family to their new home in Beverly.

Mary Louise now found she must "get acquainted" with Mamma Bee and Gran'pa Jim all over again, for during these last three years she had developed so fast in mind and body that her previous knowledge of her relatives seemed like a hazy dream. The Colonel also discovered a new granddaughter, to whom he became passionately attached. For two years now they had grown together until they were great friends and cronies.

As for Mrs Burrows, she seemed to have devoted her whole life to her father, the Colonel. She had lost much of her former beauty and had become a thin, pale woman with anxious eyes and an expectant and deprecating air, as if always prepared to ward off a sudden blow. Her solicitude for the old Colonel was almost pathetic and while he was in her presence she constantly hovered around him, doing little things for his comfort which he invariably acknowledged with his courtly bow and a gracious word of thanks.

It was through her association with this cultured old gentleman that Mary Louise had imbibed a certain degree of logic and philosophy unknown to many girls of fifteen. He taught her consideration for others as the keynote of happiness, yet he himself declined to mingle with his fellow men. He abhorred sulking and was always cheerful and pleasant in his home circle, yet when others approached him familiarly he resented it with a frown. He taught his granddaughter to be generous to the poor and supplied her freely with money for charity, yet he personally refused all demands upon him by churches or charitable societies.

In their long talks together he displayed an intimate acquaintance with men and affairs, but never referred in any way to his former life.

"Are you really a colonel?" Mary Louise once asked him.

"Men call me so," he replied, but there was a tone in his voice that warned the girl not to pursue the subject further. She knew his moods almost as well as her mother did.

The Colonel was very particular as to dress. He obtained his own clothing from a New York tailor and took a keen interest in the gowns of his daughter and of Mary Louise, his taste in female apparel being so remarkable that they were justly considered the best dressed women in Beverly. The house they were living in contained an excellent library and was furnished in a quaint, old-fashioned manner that was very appealing to them all. Mary Louise sincerely hoped there would be no more changes in their lives and that they might continue to live in Beverly for many years to come.

III

A SURPRISE

On the afternoon when our story begins, Mary Louise walked home from school and found Colonel Weatherby waiting for her in the garden, leggings strapped to his gaunt legs, the checked walking-cap on his head, a gold-headed crop in his hand.

"Let us go for a walk, my dear," he proposed. "It is Friday, so you will have all day tomorrow in which to get your lessons."

"Oh, it won't take all day for that," she replied with a laugh. "I'll be glad of the walk. Where shall we go, Gran'pa Jim?"

"Perhaps to the mill-race. We haven't visited it for a long time."

She ran to the house to put away her books and get her stout shoes, and presently rejoined him, when together they strolled up the street and circled round the little town until they came to the river bank. Then they followed the stream toward the old mill.

Mary Louise told her grandfather of the recent edict of Miss Stearne and the indignation it had aroused in her girl boarders.

"And what do you think of it, Gran'pa Jim?" she asked in conclusion.

"What do YOU think of it, Mary Louise?"

"It is rather hard on the girls, who have enjoyed their liberty for so long; but I think it is Miss Stearne's plan to keep them away from the picture theatre."

"And so?"

"And so," she said, "it may do the girls more good than harm."

He smiled approvingly. It was his custom to draw out her ideas on all questions, rather than to assert his own in advance. If he found her wrong or misinformed he would then correct her and set her right.

"So you do not approve of the pictures, Mary Louise?"

"Not all of them, Gran'pa Jim, although they all seem to have been 'passed by the Board of Censors'—perhaps when their eyes were shut. I love the good pictures, and I know that you do, but some we have seen lately gave me the shivers. So, perhaps Miss Stearne is right."

"I am confident she is," he agreed. "Some makers of pictures may consider it beneficial to emphasize good by exhibiting evil, by way of contrast, but they are doubtless wrong. I've an old-fashioned notion that young girls should be shielded, as much as possible, from knowledge of the world's sins and worries, which is sure to be impressed upon them in later years. We cannot ignore evil, unfortunately, but we can often avoid it."

"But why, if these pictures are really harmful, does Mr Welland exhibit them at his theatre?" asked the girl.

"Mr Welland is running his theatre to make money," explained the Colonel, "and the surest way to make money is to cater to the tastes of his patrons, the majority of whom demand picture plays of the more vivid sort, such as you and I complain of. So the fault lies not with the exhibitor but with the sensation-loving public. If Mr Welland showed only such pictures as have good morals he would gain the patronage of Miss Stearne's twelve young ladies, and a few others, but the masses would refuse to support him."

"Then," said Mary Louise, "the masses ought to be educated to desire better things."

"Many philanthropists have tried to do that, and signally failed. I believe the world is gradually growing better, my dear, but ages will pass before mankind attains a really wholesome mental atmosphere. However, we should each do our humble part toward the moral uplift of our fellows and one way is not to condone what we know to be wrong."

He spoke earnestly, in a conversational tone that robbed his words of preachment. Mary Louise thought Gran'pa Jim must be an exceptionally good man and hoped she would grow, in time, to be like him. The only thing that puzzled her was why he refused to associate with his fellow men, while at heart he so warmly espoused their uplift and advancement.

They had now reached the mill-race and had seated themselves on the high embankment where they could watch the water swirl swiftly beneath them. The mill was not grinding today and its neighborhood seemed quite deserted. Here the old Colonel and his granddaughter sat dreamily for a long time, conversing casually on various subjects or allowing themselves to drift into thought. It was a happy hour for them both and was only interrupted when Jackson the miller passed by on his way home from the village. The man gave the Colonel a surly nod, but he smiled on Mary Louise, the girl being as popular in the district as her grandfather was unpopular.

After Jackson had passed them by Gran'pa Jim rose slowly and proposed they return home.

"If we go through the village," said he, "we shall reach home, without hurrying ourselves, in time to dress for dinner. I object to being hurried, don't you, Mary Louise?"

"Yes, indeed, if it can be avoided."

Going through the village saved them half a mile in distance, but Mary Louise would not have proposed it herself, on account of the Colonel's well-known aversion to meeting

A SURPRISE

people. This afternoon, however, he made the proposal himself, so they strolled away to the main road that led through the one business street of the little town.

At this hour there was little life in Beverly's main street. The farmers who drove in to trade had now returned home; the town women were busy getting supper and most of their men were at home feeding the stock or doing the evening chores. However, they passed an occasional group of two or three and around the general store stood a few other natives, listlessly awaiting the call to the evening meal. These cast curious glances at the well-known forms of the old man and the young girl, for his two years' residence had not made the testy old Colonel any less strange to them. They knew all about him there was to know—which was nothing at all—and understood they must not venture to address him as they would have done any other citizen.

Cooper's Hotel, a modest and not very inviting frame building, stood near the center of the village and as Mary Louise and her grandfather passed it the door opened and a man stepped out and only avoided bumping into them by coming to a full stop. They stopped also, of necessity, and Mary Louise was astonished to find the stranger staring into the Colonel's face with an expression of mingled amazement and incredulity on his own.

"James Hathaway, by all the gods!" he exclaimed, adding in wondering tones: "And after all these years!"

Mary Louise, clinging to her grandfather's arm, cast an upward glance at his face. It was tensely drawn; the eyelids were half closed and through their slits the Colonel's eyes glinted fiercely.

"You are mistaken, fellow. Out of my way!" he said, and seizing the girl's arm, which she had withdrawn in affright, he marched straight ahead. The man fell back, but stared after them with his former expression of bewildered surprise. Mary

Louise noted this in a glance over her shoulder and something in the stranger's attitude—was it a half veiled threat?—caused her to shudder involuntarily.

The Colonel strode on, looking neither to right nor left, saying never a word. They reached their home grounds, passed up the path in silence and entered the house. The Colonel went straight to the stairs and cried in a loud voice:

"Beatrice!"

The tone thrilled Mary Louise with a premonition of evil. A door was hastily opened and her mother appeared at the head of the stairs, looking down on them with the customary anxiety on her worn features doubly accentuated.

"Again, father?" she asked in a voice that slightly trembled.

"Yes. Come with me to the library, Beatrice."

IV

SHIFTING SANDS

Mary Louise hid herself in the drawing-room, where she could watch the closed door of the library opposite. At times she trembled with an unknown dread; again, she told herself that no harm could possibly befall her dear, good Gran'pa Jim or her faithful, loving mother. Yet why were they closeted in the library so long, and how could the meeting with that insolent stranger affect Colonel Weatherby so strongly?

After a long time her mother came out, looking more pallid and harassed than ever but strangely composed. She kissed Mary Louise, who came to meet her, and said:

"Get ready for dinner, dear. We are late."

The girl went to her room, dazed and uneasy. At dinner her mother appeared at the table, eating little or nothing, but Gran'pa Jim was not present. Afterward she learned that he had gone over to Miss Stearne's School for Girls, where he completed important arrangements concerning his granddaughter.

When dinner was over Mary Louise went into the library and, drawing a chair to where the light of the student lamp flooded her book, tried to read. But the words were blurred and her mind was in a sort of chaos. Mamma Bee had summoned Aunt Polly and Uncle Eben to her room, where she was now holding a conference with the faithful servants. A strange and subtle atmosphere of unrest pervaded the house; Mary Louise scented radical changes in their heretofore pleasant home life, but what these changes were to be or what necessitated them she could not imagine.

After a while she heard Gran'pa Jim enter the hall and hang up his hat and coat and place his cane in the rack. Then he came to the door of the library and stood a moment looking hard at Mary Louise. Her own eyes regarded her grandfather earnestly, questioning him as positively as if she had spoken.

He drew a chair before her and leaning over took both her hands in his and held them fast.

"My dear," he said gently, "I regret to say that another change has overtaken us. Have you ever heard of 'harlequin fate'? 'Tis a very buffoon of mischief and irony that is often permitted to dog our earthly footsteps and prevent us from becoming too content with our lot. For a time you and I, little maid, good comrades though we have been, must tread different paths. Your mother and I are going away, presently, and we shall leave you here in Beverly, where you may continue your studies under the supervision of Miss Stearne, as a boarder at her school. This house, although the rental is paid for six weeks longer, we shall at once vacate, leaving Uncle Eben and Aunt Sallie to put it in shape and close it properly. Do you understand all this, Mary Louise?"

"I understand what you have told me, Gran'pa Jim. But why—"

"Miss Stearne will be supplied with ample funds to cover your tuition and to purchase any supplies you may need. You will have nothing to worry about and so may devote all your energies to your studies."

"But how long—"

"Trust me and your mother to watch over your welfare, for you are very dear to us, believe me," he continued, disregarding her interruptions. "Do you remember the address of the Conants, at Dorfield?"

"Of course."

"Well, you may write to me, or to your mother, once a week, addressing the letter in care of Peter Conant. But if you are questioned by anyone," he added, gravely, "do not mention the address of the Conants or hint that I have gone to Dorfield. Write your letters privately and unobserved, in your own room, and post them secretly, by your own hand, so that no one will be aware of the correspondence. Your caution in this regard will be of great service to your mother and me. Do you think you can follow these instructions?"

"To be sure I can, Gran'pa Jim. But why must I—"

"Some day," said he, "you will understand this seeming mystery and be able to smile at your present perplexities. There is nothing to fear, my dear child, and nothing that need cause you undue anxiety. Keep a brave heart and, whatever happens, have faith in Gran'pa Jim. Your mother—as good a woman as God ever made—believes in me, and she knows all. Can you accept her judgment, Mary Louise? Can you steadfastly ignore any aspersions that may be cast upon my good name?"

"Yes, Gran'pa Jim."

She had not the faintest idea what he referred to. Not until afterward was she able to piece these strange remarks together and make sense of them. Just now the girl was most impressed by the fact that her mother and grandfather were going away and would leave her as a boarder with Miss Stearne. The delightful home life, wherein she had passed the happiest two years of her existence, was to be broken up for good and all.

"Now I must go to your mother. Kiss me, my dear!"

As he rose to his feet Mary Louise also sprang from her chair and the Colonel folded his arms around her and for a moment held her tight in his embrace. Then he slowly released her, holding the girl at arms' length while he studied her troubled face with grave intensity. One kiss upon her upturned forehead and the old man swung around and left the room without another word.

Mary Louise sank into her chair, a little sob in her throat. She felt very miserable, indeed, at that moment. "Harlequin fate!" she sighed. "I wonder why it has chosen us for its victims?"

After an hour passed in the deserted library she stole away to her own room and prepared for bed. In the night, during her fitful periods of sleep, she dreamed that her mother bent over her and kissed her lips—once, twice, a third time.

The girl woke with a start. A dim light flooded her chamber, for outside was a full moon. But the room was habited only by shadows, save for her own feverish, restless body. She turned over to find a cooler place and presently fell asleep again.

V

OFFICIAL INVESTIGATION

"And you say they are gone?" cried Mary Louise in surprise, as she came down to breakfast the next morning and found the table laid for one and old Eben waiting to serve her.

"In de night, chile. I don' know 'zac'ly wha' der time, by de clock, but de Kun'l an' Missy Burrows did'n' sleep heah a-tall."

"There is no night train," said the girl, seating herself thoughtfully at the table. "How could they go, Uncle?"

"Jus' took deh auto'bile, chile, an' de Kun'l done druv it heself—bag an' baggage. But—see heah, Ma'y 'Ouise—we-all ain' s'pose to know nuth'n' bout dat git-away. Ef some imper'nent puss'n' ask us, we ain' gwine t' know how dey go, nohow. De Kun'l say tell Ma'y 'Ouise she ain' gwine know noth'n' a-tall, 'bout nuth'n', 'cause 'tain't nobody's business."

"I understand, Uncle Eben."

She reflected upon this seemingly unnecessary secrecy as she ate her breakfast. After a time she asked:

"What are you and Aunt Polly going to do, Uncle?"

"Fus' thing," replied the old negro, "Polly gwine git yo' traps all pack up an' I gwine take 'em ovah to Missy Stearne's place in de wheel-barrer. Den I gwine red up de house an' take de keys to Mass' Gimble, de agent. Den Polly an' me we go back to our own li'l' house in de lane yondeh. De Kun'l done 'range ev'thing propeh, an' we gwine do jus' like he say."

Mary Louise felt lonely and uncomfortable in the big house, now that her mother and grandfather had gone away. Since the move was inevitable, she would be glad to go to Miss Stearne as soon as possible. She helped Aunt Polly pack her trunk and suitcase, afterwards gathering into a bundle the things she had forgotten or overlooked, all of which personal belongings Uncle Eben wheeled over to the school. Then she bade the faithful servitors goodbye, promising to call upon them at their humble home, and walked slowly over the well-known path to Miss Stearne's establishment, where she presented herself to the principal.

It being Saturday, Miss Stearne was seated at a desk in her own private room, where she received Mary Louise and bade her sit down.

Miss Stearne was a woman fifty years of age, tall and lean, with a deeply lined face and a tendency to nervousness that was increasing with her years. She was a very clever teacher and a very incompetent business woman, so that her small school, of excellent standing and repute, proved difficult to finance. In character Miss Stearne was temperamental enough to have been a genius. She was kindly natured, fond of young girls and cared for her pupils with motherly instincts seldom possessed by those in similar positions. She was lax in many respects, severely strict in others. Not always were her rules and regulations dictated by good judgment. Therefore her girls usually found as much fault as other boarding school girls are prone to do, and with somewhat more reason. On the other hand, no one could question the principal's erudition or her skill in imparting her knowledge to others.

"Sit down, Mary Louise," she said to the girl. "This is an astonishing change in your life, is it not? Colonel Weatherby came to me last evening and said he had been suddenly called away on important matters that would brook no delay, and that your mother was to accompany him on the journey. He begged me to take you in as a regular boarder and of course I consented. You have been one of my most tractable and conscientious pupils and I have been proud of your progress. But the school is quite full, as you know; so at first I was uncertain that I could accommodate you here; but Miss Dandler, my assistant, has given up her room to you and I shall put a bed for her in my own sleeping chamber, so that difficulty is now happily arranged. I suppose your family left Beverly this morning, by the early train?"

"They have gone," replied Mary Louise, non-committally.

"You will be lonely for a time, of course, but presently you will feel quite at home in the school because you know all of my girls so well. It is not like a strange girl coming into a new school. And remember, Mary Louise, that you are to come to me for any advice and assistance you need, for I promised your grandfather that I would fill your mother's place as far as I am able to do so."

Mary Louise reflected, with a little shock of pain, that her mother had never been very near to her and that Miss Stearne might well perform such perfunctory duties as the girl had been accustomed to expect. But no one could ever take the place of Gran'pa Jim.

"Thank you, Miss Stearne," she said. "I am sure I shall be quite contented here. Is my room ready?"

"Yes; and your trunk has already been placed in it. Let me know, my dear, if there is anything you need."

Mary Louise went to her room and was promptly pounced upon by Dorothy Knerr and Sue Finley, who roomed just across the hall from her and were delighted to find she was to become a regular boarder. They asked numerous questions as they helped her to unpack and settle her room, but accepted her conservative answers without comment.

At the noon luncheon Mary Louise was accorded a warm reception by the assembled boarders and this cordial welcome by her school-mates did much to restore the girl to her normal condition of cheerfulness. She even joined a group in a game of tennis after luncheon and it was while she was playing that little Miss Dandler came with a message that Mary Louise was wanted in Miss Stearne's room at once.

"Take my racquet," she said to Jennie Allen; "I'll be back in a minute."

When she entered Miss Stearne's room she was surprised to find herself confronted by the same man whom she and her grandfather had encountered in front of Cooper's Hotel the previous afternoon—the man whom she secretly held responsible for this abrupt change in her life. The principal sat crouched over her desk as if overawed by her visitor, who stopped his nervous pacing up and down the room as the girl appeared.

"This is Mary Louise Burrows," said Miss Stearne, in a weak voice.

"Huh!" He glared at her with a scowl for a moment and then demanded:

"Where's Hathaway?"

Mary Louise reddened.

"I do not know to whom you refer," she answered quietly.

"Aren't you his granddaughter?"

"I am the granddaughter of Colonel James Weatherby, sir."

"It's all the same; Hathaway or Weatherby, the scoundrel can't disguise his personality. Where is he?"

She did not reply. Her eyes had narrowed a little, as the Colonel's were sometimes prone to do, and her lips were pressed firmly together.

"Answer me!" he shouted, waving his arms threateningly.

"Miss Stearne," Mary Louise said, turning to the principal, "unless you request your guest to be more respectful I shall leave the room."

"Not yet you won't," said the man in a less boisterous tone. "Don't annoy me with your airs, for I'm in a hurry. Where is Hathaway—or Weatherby—or whatever he calls himself?"

"I do not know."

"You don't, eh? Didn't he leave an address?"

"No."

"I don't believe you. Where did he go?"

"If I knew," said Mary Louise with dignity, "I would not inform you."

He uttered a growl and then threw back his coat, displaying a badge attached to his vest.

"I'm a federal officer," he asserted with egotistic pride, "a member of the Government's Secret Service Department. I've been searching for James J. Hathaway for nine years, and so has every man in the service. Last night I stumbled upon him by accident, and on inquiring found he has been living quietly in this little jumping-off place. I wired the Department for instructions and an hour ago received orders to arrest him, but found my bird had flown. He left you behind, though, and I'm wise to the fact that you're a clew that will lead me straight to him. You're going to do that very thing, and the sooner you make up your mind to it the better for all of us. No nonsense, girl! The Federal Government's not to be trifled with. Tell me where to find your grandfather."

"If you have finished your insolent remarks," she answered with spirit, "I will go away. You have interrupted my game of tennis."

He gave a bark of anger that made her smile, but as she turned away he sprang forward and seized her arm, swinging her around so that she again faced him.

"Great Caesar, girl! Don't you realize what you're up against?" he demanded.

"I do," said she. "I seem to be in the power of a brute. If a law exists that permits you to insult a girl, there must also be a law to punish you. I shall see a lawyer and try to have you properly punished for this absolute insolence."

He regarded her keenly, still frowning, but when he spoke again he had moderated both his tone and words.

"I do not intend to be insolent, Miss Burrows, but I have been greatly aggravated by your grandfather's unfortunate escape and in this emergency every moment is precious if I am to capture him before he gets out of America, as he has done once or twice before. Also, having wired the Department that I have found Hathaway, I shall be discredited if I let him slip through my fingers, so I am in a desperate fix. If I have seemed a bit gruff and nervous, forgive me. It is your duty, as a loyal subject of the United States, to assist an officer of the law by every means in your power, especially when he is engaged in running down a criminal. Therefore, whether you dislike to or not, you must tell me where to find your grandfather."

"My grandfather is not a criminal, sir."

"The jury will decide that when his case comes to trial. At present he is accused of crime and a warrant is out for his arrest. Where is he?"

"I do not know," she persisted.

"He—he left by the morning train, which goes west," stammered Miss Stearne, anxious to placate the officer and fearful of the girl's stubborn resistance.

"So the servant told me," sneered the man; "but he didn't. I was at the station myself—two miles from this forsaken place—to make sure that Hathaway didn't skip while I was waiting for orders. Therefore, he is either hidden somewhere in Beverly or he has sneaked away to an adjoining town. The old serpent is slippery as an eel; but I'm going to catch him, this time, as sure as fate, and this girl must give me all the information she can."

"Oh, that will be quite easy," retorted Mary Louise, somewhat triumphantly, "for I have no information to divulge."

He began to pace the room again, casting at her shrewd and uncertain glances.

"He didn't say where he was going?"

"No."

"Or leave any address?"

"No."

"What DID he say?"

"That he was going away and would arrange with Miss Stearne for me to board at the school."

"Huh! I see. Foxy old guy. Knew I would question you and wouldn't take chances. If he writes you, or you learn what has become of him, will you tell me?"

"No."

"I thought not." He turned toward the principal. "How about this girl's board money?" he asked. "When did he say he'd send it?"

"He paid me in advance, to the end of the present term," answered the agitated Miss Stearne.

"Foxy old boy! Seemed to think of everything. I'm going, now; but take this warning—both of you. Don't gabble about what I've said. Keep the secret. If nothing gets out, Hathaway may think the coast is clear and it's safe for him to come back. In that case I—or someone appointed by the Department—will get a chance to nab him. That's all. Good day."

He made his exit from the room without ceremony, leaving Mary Louise and Miss Stearne staring fearfully at one another.

"It—it's—dreadful!" stammered the teacher, shrinking back with a moan.

"It would be, if it were true," said the girl. "But Gran'pa Jim is no criminal, we all know. He's the best man that ever lived, and the whole trouble is that this foolish officer has mistaken him for someone else. I heard him, with my own ears, tell the man he was mistaken."

Miss Stearne reflected.

"Then why did your grandfather run away?" she asked.

It was now Mary Louise's turn to reflect, seeking an answer. Presently she realized that a logical explanation of her grandfather's action was impossible with her present knowledge.

"I cannot answer that question, Miss Stearne," she admitted, candidly, "but Gran'pa Jim must have had some good reason."

There was unbelief in the woman's eyes—unbelief and a horror of the whole disgraceful affair that somehow included Mary Louise in its scope. The girl read this look and it confused her. She mumbled an excuse and fled to her room to indulge in a good cry.

VI

UNDER A CLOUD

The officer's injunction not to talk of the case of Colonel Weatherby was of little avail in insuring secrecy. Oscar Dowd, who owned and edited the one weekly newspaper in town, which appeared under the title of "The Beverly Beacon," was a very ferret for news. He had to be; otherwise there never would have been enough happenings in the vicinity to fill the scant columns of his little paper, which was printed in big type to make the items and editorials fill as much space as possible.

Uncle Eben met the editor and told him the Colonel had gone away suddenly and had vacated the Vandeventer mansion and put Mary Louise with Miss Stearne to board. Thereat, Oscar Dowd scented "news" and called on Miss Stearne for further information. The good lady was almost as much afraid of an editor as of an officer of the law, so under Oscar's rapid-fire questioning she disclosed more of the dreadful charge against Colonel Weatherby than she intended to. She even admitted the visit of the secret service agent, but declined to give details of it.

Oscar found the agent had departed for parts unknown—perhaps to trail the escaped Colonel—but the hotel keeper furnished him with other wisps of information and, bunching all the rumors together and sifting the wheat from the chaff, the editor evolved a most thrilling tale to print in the Wednesday paper. Some of the material his own imagination supplied; much else was obtained from irresponsible gossips who had no foundation for their assertions. Miss Stearne was horrified to find, on receiving her copy of the Wednesday "Beacon" that big headlines across the front page announced: "Beverly Harbors a Criminal in Disguise! Flight of Colonel James Weatherby when a Federal Officer Seeks to Arrest him for a Terrible Crime!"

Then followed a mangled report of the officer's visit to Beverly on government business, his recognition of Colonel Weatherby—who was none other than the noted criminal, James J. Hathaway—on the street in front of Cooper's Hotel, how the officer wired Washington for instructions and how Hathaway, alias Weatherby, escaped in the dead of night and had so far successfully eluded all pursuit. What crime Hathaway, alias Weatherby, was accused of, the officer would not divulge, and the statements of others disagreed. One report declared the Colonel had wrecked a New York bank and absconded with enormous sums he had embezzled; another stated he had been president of a swindling stock corporation which had used the mails illegally to further its nefarious schemes. A third account asserted he had insured his life for a million dollars in favor of his daughter, Mrs Burrows, and then established a false death and reappeared after Mrs Burrows had collected the insurance money.

Having printed all this prominently in big type, the editor appended a brief note in small type saying he would not vouch for the truth of any statement made in the foregoing article. Nevertheless, it was a terrible arraignment and greatly shocked the good citizens of Beverly.

Miss Stearne, realizing how humiliated Mary Louise would be if the newspaper fell into her hands, carefully hid her copy away where none of the girls could see it; but one of the day scholars brought a copy to the school Thursday morning and passed it around among the girls, so that all were soon in possession of the whole scandalous screed.

Mable Westervelt, after feasting upon the awful accusations, cruelly handed the paper to Mary Louise. The girl's face blanched and then grew red, her mouth fell open as if gasping for breath and her eyes stared with a pained, hopeless expression at the printed page that branded her dearly loved Gran'pa Jim a swindler and a thief. She rose quickly and left the room, to the great relief of the other girls, who wanted to talk the matter over.

"The idea," cried Mable indignantly, "of that old villain's foisting his grandchild on this respectable school while he ran away to escape the penalty of his crimes!"

"Mary Louise is all right," asserted Jennie Allen stoutly. "She isn't to blame, at all."

"I warned you that her goody-goody airs were a cloak to hidden wickedness," said Mable, tossing her head.

"Blood will tell," drawled Lina Darrow, a very fat girl. "Mary Louise has bad blood in her veins and it's bound to crop out, sooner or later. I advise you girls to keep your trunks locked and to look after your jewelry."

"Shame—shame!" cried Dorothy Knerr, and the others echoed the reproach. Even Mable looked at fat Lina disapprovingly.

However, in spite of staunch support on the part of her few real friends, Mary Louise felt from that hour a changed atmosphere when in the presence of her school fellows. Weeks rolled by without further public attacks upon Gran'pa Jim, but among the girls at the school suspicion had crept in to ostracize Mary Louise from the general confidence. She lost her bright, cheery air of self-assurance and grew shy and fearful of reproach, avoiding her schoolmates more than they avoided her. Instead of being content in her new home, as she had hoped to be, the girl found herself more miserable and discontented than at any other period of her life. She longed continually to be comforted by Gran'pa Jim and Mamma Bee, and even lost interest in her studies, moping dismally in her room when she should have been taking an interest in the life at the school.

Even good Miss Stearne had unconsciously changed in her attitude toward the forlorn girl. Deciding one day that she needed some new shoes, Mary Louise went to the principal to ask for the money with which to buy them.

Miss Stearne considered the matter seriously. Then she said with warning emphasis:

"My dear, I do not think it advisable for you to waste your funds on shoes, especially as those you have are in fairly good condition. Of course, your grandfather left some money with me, to be expended as I saw fit, but now that he has abscon—eh—eh—secreted himself, so to speak, we can expect no further remittances. When this term is ended any extra money should be applied toward your further board and tuition. Otherwise you would become an outcast, with no place to go and no shelter for your head. That, in common decency, must be avoided. No; I do not approve of any useless expenditures. I shall hoard this money for future emergencies."

In happier times Mary Louise would have been indignant at the thought that her grandfather would ever leave her unprovided for, but she had been so humbled of late that this aspect of her affairs, so candidly presented by Miss Stearne, troubled her exceedingly. She had written a letter every week to her grandfather, addressing it, as he had instructed her to do, in care of Mr Peter Conant at Dorfield. And always she had stolen out, unobserved, and mailed the letter at the village post office. Of course she had never by a single word referred to the scandal regarding the Colonel or her mother, or to her own unhappy lot at school because of that scandal, knowing how such a report would grieve them; but the curious thing about this correspondence was that it was distinctly one-sided. In the three months since they had gone away, Mary Louise had never received an answer to any of her letters, either from her grandfather or her mother.

This might be explained, she reflected, by the fact that they suspected the mails would be watched; but this supposition attributed some truth to the accusation that Gran'pa Jim was a fugitive from justice, which she would not allow for an instant. Had he not told her to have faith in him, whatever happened? Should she prove disloyal just because a brutal officer and an irresponsible newspaper editor had branded her dear grandfather a criminal?

No! Whatever happened she would cling to her faith in the goodness of dear Gran'pa Jim.

There was very little money in her purse; a few pennies that she must hoard to buy postage stamps with. Two parties for young people were given in Beverly and at both of them Mary Louise was the only girl boarding at the school who was uninvited. She knew that some of the girls even resented her presence at the school and often when she joined a group of schoolmates their hushed conversation warned her they had been discussing her.

Altogether, she felt that her presence at the school was fast becoming unbearable and when one of the boarders openly accused her of stealing a diamond ring—which was later discovered on a shelf above a washstand—the patient humility of Mary Louise turned to righteous anger and she resolved to leave the shelter of Miss Stearne's roof without delay.

There was only one possible place for her to go—to the Conant house at Dorfield, where her mother and grandfather were staying and where she had already passed three of the most pleasant years of her short life. Gran'pa Jim had not told her she could come to him, even in an emergency, but when she explained all the suffering she had endured at the school she knew quite well that he would forgive her for coming.

But she needed money for the long journey, and this must be secured in some way from her own resources. So she got together all the jewelry she possessed and placing it in her handbag started for the town.

She had an idea that a jewelry shop was the proper place to sell her jewelry, but Mr Trumbull the jeweler shook his head and said that Watson, at the bank, often loaned money on such security. He advised the girl to see Watson.

So Mary Louise went to the "bank," which was a one-man affair situated in the rear of the hardware store, where a grating had been placed in one corner. There she found Mr Watson, who was more a country broker than a banker, and throve by lending money to farmers.

Gran'pa Jim was almost as fond of pretty jewels as he was of good clothes and he had always been generous in presenting his granddaughter with trinkets on her birthdays and at Christmas time. The jewelry she laid before Mr Watson was really valuable and the banker's eye was especially attracted by a brooch of pearls that must have cost several hundred dollars.

"How much do you want to borrow on this lot?" he asked.

"As much as I can get, sir," she replied.

"Have you any idea of redeeming it?"

"I hope to do so, of course."

The banker knew perfectly well who Mary Louise was and suspected she needed money.

"This is no pawnbroker's shop," he asserted. "I'll give you a hundred dollars, outright, for this pearl brooch—as a purchase, understand—but the rest of the junk I don't want."

A little man who had entered the hardware store to purchase a tin dipper was getting so close to the "bank" that Mary Louise feared being overheard; so she did not argue with Mr Watson. Deciding that a hundred dollars ought to take her to

Dorfield, she promptly accepted the offer, signed a bill of sale and received her money. Then she walked two miles to the railway station and discovered that a ticket to Dorfield could be bought for ninety-two dollars. That would give her eight dollars leeway, which seemed quite sufficient. Elated at the prospect of freedom she returned to the school to make her preparation for departure and arrived just in time to join the other girls at dinner.

VII

THE ESCAPE

As she packed her trunk behind the locked door of her room—an unnecessary precaution, since the girls generally avoided her society—Mary Louise considered whether to confide the fact of her going to Miss Stearne or to depart without a word of adieu. In the latter case she would forfeit her trunk and her pretty clothes, which she did not wish to do unless it proved absolutely necessary; and, after all, she decided, frankness was best. Gran'pa Jim had often said that what one could not do openly should not be done at all. There was nothing to be ashamed of in her resolve to leave the school where she was so unhappy. The girls did not want her there and she did not want to stay; the school would be relieved of a disturbing element and Mary Louise would be relieved of unjust persecution; no blame attached to any but those who had made public this vile slander against her grandfather. From all viewpoints she considered she was doing the right thing; so, when her preparations were complete, she went to Miss Stearne's room, although it was now after eight o'clock in the evening, and requested an interview.

"I am going away," she quietly announced to the principal.

"Going away! But where?" asked the astonished teacher.

"I cannot tell you that, Miss Stearne."

"Do you not know?"

"Yes, I know, but I prefer not to tell you."

Miss Stearne was greatly annoyed. She was also perplexed. The fact that Mary Louise was deserting her school did not seem so important, at the moment, as the danger involved by a young girl's going out into the world unprotected. The good woman had already been rendered very nervous by the dreadful accusation of Colonel Weatherby and the consequent stigma that attached to his granddaughter, a pupil at her eminently respectable school. She realized perfectly that the girl was blameless, whatever her grandsire might have done, and she deeply deplored the scornful attitude assumed by the other pupils toward poor Mary Louise; nevertheless a certain bitter resentment of the unwholesome scandal that had smirched her dignified establishment had taken possession of the woman, perhaps unconsciously, and while she might be a little ashamed of the ungenerous feeling, Miss Stearne fervently wished she had never accepted the girl as a pupil.

She HAD accepted her, however. She had received the money for Mary Louise's tuition and expenses and had promptly applied the entire sum to reducing her grocery bills and other pressing obligations; therefore she felt it her duty to give value received. If Mary Louise was to be driven from the school by the jeers and sneers of the other girls, Miss Stearne would feel like a thief. Moreover, it would be a distinct reproach to her should she allow a fifteen-year-old girl to wander into a cruel world because her school—her sole home and refuge—had been rendered so unbearable that she could not remain there. The principal was really unable to repay the money that had been advanced to her, even if that would relieve her of obligation to shelter the girl, and therefore she decided that Mary Louise must not be permitted, under any circumstances, to leave her establishment without the authority of her natural guardians.

This argument ran hurriedly through her mind as the girl stood calmly waiting.

"Is this action approved by your mother, or—or—by your grandfather?" she asked, somewhat more harshly than was her wont in addressing her pupils.

"No, Miss Stearne."

"Then how dare you even suggest it?"

"I am not wanted here," returned the girl with calm assurance. "My presence is annoying to the other girls, as well as to yourself, and so disturbs the routine of the school. For my part, I—I am very unhappy here, as you must realize, because everyone seems to think my dear Gran'pa Jim is a wicked man—which I know he is not. I have no heart to study, and—and so—it is better for us all that I go away."

This statement was so absolutely true and the implied reproach was so justified, that Miss Stearne allowed herself to become angry as the best means of opposing the girl's design.

"This is absurd!" she exclaimed. "You imagine these grievances, Mary Louise, and I cannot permit you to attack the school and your fellow boarders in so reckless a manner. You shall not stir one step from this school! I forbid you, positively, to leave the grounds hereafter without my express permission. You have been placed in my charge and I insist that you obey me. Go to your room and study your lessons, which you have been shamefully neglecting lately. If I hear any more of this rebellious wish to leave the school, I shall be obliged to punish you by confining you to your room."

The girl listened to this speech with evident surprise; yet the tirade did not seem to impress her.

"You refuse, then, to let me go?" she returned.

"I positively refuse."

"But I cannot stay here, Miss Stearne," she protested.

"You must. I have always treated you kindly—I treat all my girls well if they deserve it—but you are developing a bad disposition, Mary Louise—a most reprehensible disposition, I regret to say—and the tendency must be corrected at once. Not another word! Go to your room."

Mary Louise went to her room, greatly depressed by the interview. She looked at her trunk, made a mental inventory of its highly prized contents, and sighed. But as soon as she rejoined Gran'pa Jim, she reflected, he would send an order to have the trunk forwarded and Miss Stearne would not dare refuse. For a time she must do without her pretty gowns.

Instead of studying her text books she studied the railway time-card. She had intended asking Miss Stearne to permit her to take the five-thirty train from Beverly Junction the next morning and since the recent interview she had firmly decided to board that very train. This was not entirely due to stubbornness, for she reflected that if she stayed at the school her unhappy condition would become aggravated, instead of improving, especially since Miss Stearne had developed unexpected sharpness of temper. She would endure no longer the malicious taunts of her school fellows or the scoldings of the principal, and these could be avoided in no other way than by escaping as she had planned.

At ten o'clock she lay down upon her bed, fully dressed, and put out her light; but she dared not fall asleep lest she miss her train. At times she lighted a match and looked at her watch and it surprised her to realize how long a night can be when one is watching for daybreak.

At four o'clock she softly rose, put on her hat, took her suitcase in hand and stealthily crept from the room. It was very dark in the hallway but the house was so familiar to her that she easily felt her way along the passage, down the front stairs and so to the front door.

Miss Stearne always locked this door at night but left the key in the lock. Tonight the key had been withdrawn. When Mary Louise had satisfied herself of this fact she stole along the lower hallway toward the rear. The door that connected with the dining-room and farther on with the servants' quarters had also been locked and the key withdrawn. This was so unusual that it plainly told the girl that Miss Stearne was suspicious that she might try to escape, and so had taken precautions to prevent her leaving the house.

Mary Louise cautiously set down her suitcase and tried to think what to do. The house had not been built for a school but was an old residence converted to school purposes. On one side of the hall was a big drawing-room; on the other side were the principal's apartments.

Mary Louise entered the drawing-room and ran against a chair that stood in her way. Until now she had not made the slightest noise, but the suitcase banged against the chair and the concussion reverberated dully throughout the house.

The opposite door opened and a light flooded the hall. From where the girl stood in the dark drawing-room she could see Miss Stearne standing in her doorway and listening. Mary Louise held herself motionless. She scarcely dared breathe. The principal glanced up and down the hall, noted the locked doors and presently retired into her room, after a little while extinguishing the light.

Then Mary Louise felt her way to a window, drew aside the heavy draperies and carefully released the catch of the sash, which she then succeeded in raising. The wooden blinds were easily unfastened but swung back with a slight creak that made her heart leap with apprehension. She did not wait, now, to learn if the sound had been heard, for already she had wasted too much time if she intended to catch her train. She leaned through the window, let her suitcase down as far as she could reach, and dropped it to the ground. Then she climbed through the opening and let herself down by clinging to the sill. It was a high window, but she was a tall girl for her age and her feet touched the ground. Now she was free to go her way.

THE ESCAPE

She lost no time in getting away from the grounds, being guided by a dim starlight and a glow in the east that was a promise of morning. With rapid steps she made her way to the station, reaching it over the rough country road just as the train pulled in. She had been possessed with the idea that someone was stealthily following her and under the light of the depot lamps her first act was to swing around and stare into the darkness from which she had emerged. She almost expected to see Miss Stearne appear, but it was only a little man with a fat nose and a shabby suit of clothes, who had probably come from the village to catch the same train she wanted. He paid no attention to the girl but entered the same car she did and quietly took his seat in the rear.

VIII

A FRIENDLY FOE

It required two days and a night to go by rail from Beverly to Dorfield and as Mary Louise had passed a sleepless night at the school she decided to purchase a berth on the sleeper. That made a big hole in her surplus of eight dollars and she also found her meals in the dining car quite expensive, so that by the time she left the train at Dorfield her finances would be reduced to the sum of a dollar and twenty cents.

That would not have disturbed her, knowing that thereafter she would be with Gran'pa Jim, except for one circumstance. The little man with the fat nose, who had taken the train at Beverly, was still on board. All the other passengers who had been on the train at that time had one by one left it and been replaced by others, for the route lay through several large cities where many alighted and others came aboard. Only the little man from Beverly remained, quiet and unobtrusive but somehow haunting the girl's presence in an embarrassing manner.

He seldom looked at her but was found staring from the window whenever she turned her eyes toward him. At first she scarcely noticed the man, but the longer he remained aboard the train the more she speculated as to where he might be going. Whenever she entered the dining car he took a notion to eat at that time, but found a seat as far removed from her as possible. She imagined she had escaped him when she went to the sleeper, but next morning as she passed out he was standing in the vestibule and a few moments later he was in the diner where she was breakfasting.

It was now that the girl first conceived the idea that he might be following her for a purpose, dogging her footsteps to discover at what station she left the train. And, when she asked herself why the stranger should be so greatly concerned with her movements, she remembered that she was going to Gran'pa Jim and that at one time an officer had endeavored to discover, through her, her grandfather's whereabouts.

"If this little man," she mused, glancing at his blank, inexpressive features, "happens to be a detective, and knows who I am, he may think I will lead him directly to Colonel Weatherby, whom he may then arrest. Gran'pa Jim is innocent, of course, but I know he doesn't wish to be arrested, because he left Beverly suddenly to avoid it. And," she added with a sudden feinting of the heart, "if this suspicion is true I am actually falling into the trap and leading an officer to my grandfather's retreat."

This reflection rendered the girl very uneasy and caused her to watch the fat-nosed man guardedly all through that tedious day. She constantly hoped he would leave the train at some station and thus prove her fears to be groundless, but always he remained in his seat, patiently eyeing the landscape through his window.

Late in the afternoon another suspicious circumstance aroused her alarm. The conductor of the train, as he passed through the car, paused at the rear end and gazed thoughtfully at the little man huddled in the rear seat, who seemed unconscious of his regard. After watching him a while the conductor suddenly turned his head and looked directly at Mary Louise, with a curious expression, as if connecting his two passengers. Then he went on through the train, but the girl's heart was beating high and the little man, while seeming to eye the fleeting landscape through the window, wriggled somewhat uneasily in his seat.

Mary Louise now decided he was a detective. She suspected that he had been sent to Beverly, after the other man left, to watch her movements, with the idea that sooner or later she would rejoin her grandfather. Perhaps, had any letter come for her from her mother or Gran'pa Jim, this officer would have seized it and obtained from it the address of the man he was seeking. That would account for their failure to write her; perhaps they were aware of the plot and therefore dared not send her a letter.

And now she began wondering what she should do when she got to Dorfield, if the little man also left the train at that station. Such an act on his part would prove that her suspicions were correct, in which case she would lead him straight to her grandfather, whom she would thus deliver into the power of his merciless enemies.

No; that would not do, at all. If the man followed her from the train at Dorfield she dared not go to Peter Conant's house. Where, then, COULD she go? Had she possessed sufficient money it might be best to ride past Dorfield and pay her fare to another station; but her funds were practically exhausted. Dorfield was a much bigger town than Beverly; it was quite a large city, indeed; perhaps she could escape the supervision of the detective, in some way, and by outwitting him find herself free to seek the Conant's home. She would try this and circumstances must decide her plan of action. Always there was the chance that she misjudged the little man.

As the conductor called the station the train halted and the girl passed the rear seat, where the man had his bare head half out the open window, and descended from the car to the platform. A few others also alighted, to hurry away to the omnibuses or street car or walk to their destinations.

Mary Louise stood quite still upon the platform until the train drew out after its brief stop. It was nearly six o'clock in the evening and fast growing dark, yet she distinctly observed the fat-nosed man, who had alighted on the opposite side of the track and was now sauntering diagonally across the rails to the depot, his hands thrust deep in his pockets and his eyes turned away from Mary Louise as if the girl occupied no part of his thoughts.

But she knew better than that. Her suspicions were now fully confirmed and she sought to evade the detective in just the way any inexperienced girl might have done. Turning in the opposite direction she hastily crossed the street, putting a big building between herself and the depot, and then hurried along a cross-street. She looked back now and then and found she had not been followed; so, to insure escape, she turned another corner, giving a fearful glance over her shoulder as she did so.

This street was not so well lighted as the others had been and she had no idea where it led to. She knew Dorfield pretty well, having once resided there for three years, but in her agitated haste she had now lost all sense of direction. Feeling, however, that she was now safe from pursuit, she walked on more slowly, trying to discover her whereabouts, and presently passed a dimly-lighted bakery before which a man stood looking abstractedly into the window at the cakes and pies, his back toward her.

Instantly Mary Louise felt her heart sink. She did not need to see the man's face to recognize the detective. Nor did he stir as she passed him by and proceeded up the street. But how did he happen to be there? Had she accidentally stumbled upon him, or had he purposely placed himself in her path to assure her that escape from him was impossible?

As she reached the next corner a street car came rushing along, halted a brief moment and proceeded on its way. In that moment Mary Louise had stepped aboard and as she entered the closed section and sank into a seat she breathed a sigh of relief. The man at the bakery window had not followed her. The car made one or two more stops, turned a corner and stopped again. This time the little man with the fat nose deliberately swung himself to the rear platform, paid his fare and remained there. He didn't look at Mary Louise at all, but she looked at him and her expression was one of mingled horror and fear.

A mile farther on the car reached the end of its line and the conductor reversed the trolley-pole and prepared for the return journey. Mary Louise kept her seat. The detective watched the motorman and conductor with an assumption of stupid interest and retained his place on the platform.

On the way back to the business section of Dorfield, Mary Louise considered what to do next. She was very young and inexperienced; she was also, at this moment, very weary and despondent. It was clearly evident that she could not escape this man, whose persistence impressed her with the imminent danger that threatened her grandfather if she went to the home of the Conants—the one thing she positively must not do. Since her arrival was wholly unexpected by her friends, with whom she could not communicate, she now found herself a forlorn wanderer, without money or shelter.

When the car stopped at Main Street she got off and walked slowly along the brilliantly lighted thoroughfare, feeling more safe among the moving throngs of people. Presently she came to a well-remembered corner where the principal hotel stood on one side and the First National Bank on the other. She now knew where she was and could find the direct route to the Conants, had she dared go there. To gain time for thought the girl stepped into the doorway of the bank, which was closed for the day, thus avoiding being jostled by pedestrians. She set down her suitcase, leaned against the door-frame and tried to determine her wisest course of action.

She was hungry, tired, frightened, and the combination of sensations made her turn faint. With a white face and despair in her heart she leaned heavily back and closed her eyes.

"Pardon me," said a soft voice, and with a nervous start she opened her eyes to find the little fat-nosed man confronting her. He had removed his hat and was looking straight into her face—for the first time, she imagined—and now she noticed that his gray eyes were not at all unkindly.

"What do you want?" she asked sharply, with an involuntary shudder.

"I wish to advise you, Miss Burrows," he replied. "I believe you know who I am and it is folly for us to pursue this game of hide-and-seek any longer. You are tired and worn out with your long ride and the anxiety I have caused you."

"You are dogging me!" she exclaimed indignantly.

"I am keeping you in sight, according to orders."

"You are a detective!" she asked, a little disarmed by his frankness.

"John O'Gorman by name, Miss. At home I have a little girl much like you, but I doubt if my Josie—even though I have trained her—would prove more shrewd than you have done under such trying circumstances. Even in the train you recognized my profession—and I am thought to be rather clever at disguising my motives."

"Yes?"

"And you know quite well that because you have come to Dorfield to join your grandfather, whom you call Colonel Weatherby, I have followed you in an attempt to discover, through you, the man for whom our government has searched many years."

"Oh, indeed!"

"Therefore you are determined not to go to your destination and you are at your wits' end to know what to do. Let me advise you, for the sake of my own little Josie."

The abrupt proposal bewildered her.

"You are my enemy!"

"Don't think that, Miss," he said gently. "I am an officer of the law, engaged in doing my duty. I am not your enemy and bear you no ill-will."

"You are trying to arrest my grandfather."

"In the course of duty. But he is quite safe from me for tonight, while you are almost exhausted through your efforts to protect him. Go into the hotel across the way and register and get some supper and a room. Tomorrow you will be able to think more clearly and may then make up your mind what to do."

She hesitated. The voice seemed earnest and sincere, the eyes considerate and pitying, and the advice appealed to her as good; but—

"Just for tonight, put yourself in my care," he said. "I'm ashamed to have annoyed you to such an extent and to have interfered with your plans; but I could not help it. You have succeeded in balking the DETECTIVE, but the MAN admires you for it. I noticed, the last time you took out your purse in the dining-car, that your money is nearly gone. If you will permit me to lend you enough for your hotel expenses—"

"No."

"Well, it may not be necessary. Your friends will supply you with money whenever our little—comedy, shall we say?—is played to the end. In the meantime I'll speak to the landlord. Now, Miss Burrows, run across to the hotel and register."

She gazed at him uncertainly a moment and the little man smiled reassuringly. Somehow, she felt inclined to trust him.

"Thank you," she said and took her suitcase into the hotel office.

The clerk looked at her rather curiously as she registered, but assigned her a room and told her that dinner was still being served. She followed the bellboy to her room, where she brushed her gown, bathed her hands and face and rearranged her hair. Then she went to the dining-room and, although the journey and worry had left her sick and nervous, she ate some dinner and felt stronger and better after it.

IX

OFFICER O'GORMAN

Mary Louise returned to her room and sat down to consider the best way out of her dilemma. The detective's friendliness, so frankly expressed, pleased her, in a way, yet she realized his vigilance would not be relaxed and that he was still determined, through her, to discover where Gran'pa Jim was hidden.

An uncomfortable degree of danger had already been incurred by her unconsciously leading the officer to Dorfield. He knew now that the man he was seeking was either in this city or its immediate neighborhood. But unless she led him to the exact spot—to the dwelling of the Conants—it would take even this clever detective some time to locate the refugee. Before then Mary Louise hoped to be able to warn Gran'pa Jim of his danger. That would prevent her from rejoining him and her mother, but it would also save him from arrest.

Glancing around her comfortable room she saw a telephone on the wall. Beside it, on a hook, hung the book containing the addresses of the subscribers. She opened the book and glancing down its columns found:

"Conant, Peter; r. 1216 Oak St. Blue 147."

Why hadn't she thought of this simple method of communication before? It would be quite easy to call

Mr Conant and tell him where she was and have him warn Gran'pa Jim that a detective was searching for him.

She went to the telephone and took down the receiver.

"Office!" cried a sharp voice. "What number do you want?"

Mary Louise hesitated; then she hung up the receiver without reply. It occurred to her that the hotel office was a public place and that the telephone girl would be likely to yell out the number for all to overhear.

To satisfy herself on this point she went downstairs in the elevator and purchased a magazine at the news stand. The telephone desk was nearby and Mary Louise could hear the girl calling the numbers and responding to calls, while not six feet from her desk sat a man whose person was nearly covered by a spread newspaper which he appeared to be reading. But Mary Louise knew him by his striped trousers and straightway congratulated herself on her caution. Undoubtedly the detective had figured on her telephoning and she had nearly fallen into the trap.

Back to her room she went, resolved to make no further move till morning. The day had been a hard one for the girl, mentally and physically, and at this moment she felt herself hopelessly involved in a snare from which she could see no means of escape. She read a little in her magazine, to quiet her nerves, and then went to bed and fell asleep.

At daybreak Mary Louise wakened to wonder if she had done right in running away from Miss Stearne's school. Gran'pa Jim had placed her there because he did not wish to take her with him when he left Beverly, and now she had come to him without his consent and in doing so had perhaps delivered him into the hands of his enemies. Poor Gran'pa Jim! She would never cease to reproach herself if she became responsible for his ruin.

As she lay in bed, thinking in this vein, she allowed herself to wonder for the first time why her dear grandfather was being persecuted by the officers of the law—by the Government of the United States, indeed, which should be just and merciful to all its people. Of course he was innocent of any wrong-doing; Gran'pa Jim would never do anything to injure a human being, for he was goodness itself and had taught her to honor truth and righteousness ever since she could remember. Never for a moment would she doubt him. But it was curious, when she came to reflect upon it, that he would run away from his enemies instead of facing them bravely. For many years he had hidden himself—first in one place and then in another—and at the first warning of discovery or pursuit would disappear and seek a new hiding-place. For she now realized, in the light of her recent knowledge, that for many years Gran'pa Jim had been a fugitive from the law, and that for some unknown reason he dared not face his accusers.

Some people might consider this an evidence of guilt, but Mary Louise and Gran'pa Jim had been close comrades for two years and deep in her heart was the unalterable conviction that his very nature would revolt against crime of any sort. Moreover—always a strong argument in her mind—her mother had steadfastly believed in her grandfather and had devoted herself to him to the exclusion of all else in her life, even neglecting her own daughter to serve her father. Mamma Bee loved her, she well knew, yet Mary Louise had never enjoyed the same affectionate intercourse with her mother that she had with her grandfather, for Mamma Bee's whole life seemed to center around the old Colonel. This unusual devotion was proof enough to Mary Louise that her grandfather was innocent, but it did not untangle the maze.

Looking back over her past life, she could recall the many sudden changes of residence due to Colonel Weatherby's desire to escape apprehension by the authorities. They seemed to date from the time they had left that big city house, where the child had an especial nurse and there were lots of servants, and where her beautiful mother used to bend over her with a goodnight kiss while arrayed in dainty ball costumes sparkling with jewels. Mary Louise tried to remember her father, but could not, although she had been told that he died in that very house. She remembered Gran'pa Jim in those days, however, only he was too busy to pay much attention to her. Let's see; was he called "Colonel Weatherby" in those days! She could not recollect. That name did not become familiar to her until long afterward. Always he had been just "Gran'pa Jim" to her. Yet that dreadful officer of the law who had questioned her in Beverly had called him "Hathaway—James J. Hathaway." How absurd!

But where had she heard the name of Hathaway before? She puzzled her brain to remember. Did it belong to any of her schoolgirl friends? Or was it—

With a sudden thought she sprang from her bed and took her watch from the dresser. It was an old watch, given her by Mamma Bee on the girl's twelfth birthday, while she was living with the Conants, and her mother had bidden her to treasure it because it had belonged to her when she was a girl of Mary Louise's age. The watch was stem-winding and had a closed case, the back lid of which had seldom been opened because it fitted very tightly. But now Mary Louise pried it open with a hatpin and carried it to the light. On the inside of the gold case the following words were engraved:

"Beatrice Hathaway, from her loving Father."

Mary Louise stared at this inscription for a long while. For the first time, ugly doubts began to creep into her heart. The officer was right when he said that James Hathaway was masquerading under the false name of Colonel Weatherby. Gran'pa Jim had never told even Mary Louise that his real name was Hathaway; Mamma Bee had never told her, either. With a deep sigh she snapped the case of the watch in place and then began to dress.

It was still too early for breakfast when she had finished her toilet, so she sat by the open window of her room, looking down into the street, and tried to solve the mystery of Gran'pa Jim. Better thoughts came to her, inspiring her with new courage. Her grandfather had changed his name to enable him the more easily to escape observation, for it was James Hathaway who was accused, not Colonel James Weatherby. It was difficult, however, for the girl to familiarize herself with the idea that Gran'pa Jim was really James Hathaway; still, if her mother's name before her marriage was indeed Beatrice Hathaway, as the watch proved, then there was no question but her grandfather's name was also Hathaway. He had changed it for a purpose and she must not question the honesty of that purpose, however black the case looked against her beloved Gran'pa Jim.

This discovery, nevertheless, only added to the mystery of the whole affair, which she realized her inability to cope with. Grouping the facts with which she was familiar into regular order, her information was limited as follows:

Once Gran'pa Jim was rich and prosperous and was named Hathaway. He had many friends and lived in a handsome city house. Suddenly he left everything and ran away, changing his name to that of Weatherby. He was afraid, for some unknown reason, of being arrested, and whenever discovery threatened his retreat he would run away again. In this manner he had maintained his liberty for nine years, yet today the officers of the law seemed as anxious to find him as at first. To sum up, Gran'pa Jim was accused of a crime so important that it could not be condoned and only his cleverness in evading arrest had saved him from prison.

That would look pretty black to a stranger, and it made even Mary Louise feel very uncomfortable and oppressed, but against the accusation the girl placed these facts, better known to her than the others: Gran'pa Jim was a good man, kind and honest. Since she had known him his life had been blameless. Mamma Bee, who knew him best of all, never faltered in her devotion to him. He was incapable of doing an evil deed, he abhorred falsehood, he insisted on defending the rights of his fellow men. Therefore, in spite of any evidence against him Mary Louise believed in his innocence.

Having settled this belief firmly in mind and heart, the girl felt a distinct sense of relief. She would doubt no more. She would not try, in the future, to solve a mystery that was beyond her comprehension. Her one duty was to maintain an unfaltering faith.

At seven o'clock she went to the breakfast room, to which but two or three other guests of the hotel had preceded her, and in a few minutes Detective O'Gorman entered and seated himself at a table near her. He bowed very respectfully as he caught her eye and she returned the salutation, uneasy at the man's presence but feeling no especial antagonism toward him. As he had said, he was but doing his duty.

O'Gorman finished his breakfast before Mary Louise did, after which, rising from his chair, he came toward her table and asked quietly:

"May I sit at your table a moment, Miss Burrows?"

She neither consented nor refused, being taken by surprise, but O'Gorman sat down without requiring an answer.

"I wish to tell you," he began, "that my unpleasant espionage of you is ended. It will be needless for me to embarrass or annoy you longer."

"Indeed?"

"Yes. Aren't you glad?" with a smile at her astonished expression. "You see, I've been busy investigating while you slept. I've visited the local police station and—various other places. I am satisfied that Mr Hathaway—or Mr Weatherby, as he calls himself—is not in Dorfield and has never located here. Once again the man has baffled the entire force of our department. I am now confident that your coming to this town was not to meet your grandfather but to seek refuge with other friends, and so I have been causing you all this bother and vexation for nothing."

She looked at him in amazement.

"I'm going to ask you to forgive me," he went on, "and unless I misjudge your nature you're not going to bear any grudge against me. They sent me to Beverly to watch you, and for a time that was a lazy man's job. When you sold some of your jewelry for a hundred dollars, however, I knew there would be something doing. You were not very happy at your school, I knew, and my first thought was that you merely intended to run away—anywhere to escape the persecution of those heartless girls. But you bought a ticket for Dorfield, a faraway town, so I at once decided—wrongly, I admit—that you knew where Hathaway was and intended going to him. So I came with you, to find he is not here. He has never been here. Hathaway is too distinguished a personage, in appearance, to escape the eye of the local police. So I am about to set you free, my girl, and to return immediately to my headquarters in Washington."

She had followed his speech eagerly and with a feeling of keen disappointment at his report that her grandfather and her mother were not in Dorfield. Could it be true?

Officer O'Gorman took a card from his pocket-book and laid it beside her plate.

"My dear child," said he in a gentle tone, "I fear your life is destined to be one of trials and perplexities, if not of dreary heartaches. I have watched over you and studied your character for longer than you know and I have found much in your make-up that is interesting and admirable. You remind me a good deal of my own Josie—as good and clever a girl as ever lived. So I am going to ask you to consider me your friend. Keep this card and if ever you get into serious difficulty I want you to wire me to come and help you. If I should happen, at the time, to have duties to prevent my coming, I will send some other reliable person to your assistance. Will you promise to do this?"

"Thank you, Mr O'Gorman," she said. "I—I—your kindness embarrasses me."

"Don't allow it to do that. A detective is a man, you know, much like other men, and I have always held that the better man he is the better detective he is sure to prove. I'm obliged to do disagreeable things, at times, in the fulfillment of my duty, but I try to spare even the most hardened criminal as much as possible. So why shouldn't I be kind to a helpless, unfortunate girl?"

"Am I that?" she asked.

"Perhaps not. But I fear your grandfather's fate is destined to cause you unhappiness. You seem fond of him."

"He is the best man in all the world!"

O'Gorman looked at the tablecloth rather than to meet her eyes.

"So I will now say goodbye, Miss Burrows, and—I wish you the happiness you deserve. You're just as good a girl as my Josie is."

With this he rose to his feet and bowed again. He was a little man and he had a fat nose, but Mary Louise could not help liking him.

She was still afraid of the detective, however, and when he had left the dining-room she asked herself if his story could be true, if Gran'pa Jim was not in Dorfield—if he had never even come to the town, as O'Gorman had stated.

The Conants would know that, of course, and if the detective went away she would be free to go to the Conants for information. She would find shelter, at least, with these old friends.

As she passed from the dining-room into the hotel lobby Mr O'Gorman was paying his bill and bidding the clerk farewell. He had no baggage, except such as he might carry in his pocket, but he entered a bus that stood outside and was driven away with a final doff of his hat to the watching girl.

Mary Louise decided in the instant what to do. Mr Peter Conant was a lawyer and had an office in one of the big buildings downtown. She remembered that he always made a point of being in his office at eight o'clock in the morning, and it was nearly eight now. She would visit Mr Conant in his office, for this could not possibly endanger the safety of Gran'pa Jim in case the detective's story proved false, or if an attempt had been made to deceive her. The man had seemed sincere and for the time being he had actually gone away; but she was suspicious of detectives.

She ran upstairs for her coat and hat and at once left the hotel. She knew the way to Peter Conant's office and walked rapidly toward it.

X

RATHER QUEER INDEED

Mary Louise found the door of the office, which was located on the third floor of the Chambers Building, locked. However, the sign: "Peter Conant, Attorney at Law," was painted on the glass panel in big, distinct letters, so she was sure she had made no mistake. She slowly paced the hall, waiting, until the elevator stopped and Mr Conant stepped out and approached the door, his morning paper in one hand, a key in the other. Running to him, the girl exclaimed:

"Oh, Mr Conant!"

He stopped short and turned to face her. Then he stepped a pace backward and said:

"Great heavens, it's Mary Louise!"

"Didn't you recognize me?" she asked.

"Not at first," he answered slowly. "You have grown tall and—and—older, in two years."

"Where is Gran'pa J-"

"Hush!" with a startled glance up and down the hall. Then he unlocked the door and added: "Come in."

Mary Louise followed him through the outer office and into a smaller room beyond, the door of which Mr Conant carefully closed after them. Then he turned to look steadily at the girl, who thought he did not seem especially delighted at her appearance in Dorfield. Indeed, his first words proved this, for he asked sternly:

"Why are you here?"

"I left the school at Beverly because the girls made it so uncomfortable for me there that I could not bear it longer," she explained.

"In what way did they make it uncomfortable for you?"

"They jeered at me because—because—Gran'pa Jim is being hunted by the officers of the law, who accuse him, of doing something wicked."

Mr Conant frowned.

"Perhaps their attitude was only natural," he remarked; "but there was no accusation against you, my child. Why didn't you stick it out? The scandal would soon have died away and left you in peace."

"I was unhappy there," she said simply, "and so I thought I would come here to mother and Gran'pa Jim."

"Here?" as if surprised.

"Yes. Aren't they here, with you?"

"No."

"Then where are they?"

"I've no idea."

She sat still and stared at him, while he regarded her with a thoughtful and perplexed look on his face.

Mr Conant is difficult to describe because he was like dozens of men one meets every day, at least in outward appearance. He was neither tall nor short, lean nor fat, handsome nor ugly, attractive nor repulsive. Yet Peter Conant must not be considered a nonentity because he was commonplace in person, for he possessed mannerisms that were peculiar. He would open his eyes very wide and stare at one steadily until the person became confused and turned away. The gaze was not especially shrewd, but it was disconcerting because steadfast. When he talked he would chop off his words, one by one, with a distinct pause between each, and that often made it hard to tell whether he had ended his speech or still had more to say. When very earnest or interested he would play with a locket that dangled from his watch chain; otherwise he usually stood with his hands clasped behind his back.

Mary Louise well knew these peculiarities, having previously lived in his house, and also she knew he was a kind-hearted man, devotedly attached to his deaf wife and thoroughly trusted by Gran'pa Jim.

"I was told," said the girl presently, "to direct all my letters to my grandfather in your care."

"I am aware that you have done so," he replied.

"So I thought, of course, that he and my mother were with you."

"No; they did not come here. Colonel Weatherby arranged for me to forward your letters, which I did as soon as they arrived."

"Oh; then you know his address?"

"I do not. There are six different points to which I forward letters, in rotation, both those from you and from others on various matters of business, and these points are widely scattered. My impression is that Colonel Weatherby is in none of these places and that the letters are again forwarded to him to—wherever he may be."

Mary Louise felt quite discouraged. With hesitation she asked:

"Do you suppose you could find him for me?"

"It is impossible."

"What am I to do, Mr Conant?"

"I advise you to go back to your school."

"Can't I stay here, with you?"

He stared at her with his round eyes, playing with his locket.

"I haven't the money for the return trip," she went on falteringly. "I had to sell some of my jewelry to get here. I won't be much trouble, if you will let me live with you until I can find Gran'pa Jim."

Mr Conant still stared.

"I'm sure," said Mary Louise, "that my grandfather will gladly repay you any money it costs you to keep me."

"You—don't—un-der-stand," he retorted, chopping off his words rather viciously. "Moreover, you can't understand. Go to the house and talk to Hannah. Have you any baggage!"

"I've a suitcase at the hotel," she said, and went on to tell him the experiences of her journey and of her encounter with Detective O'Gorman.

During this relation, which he did not interrupt, Mr Conant toyed persistently with his watch charm. His features were noncommittal but he was thoroughly interested.

"You see," he remarked when she had finished, "Colonel Weatherby's elaborate system of evading discovery is quite necessary."

"But why should he wish to hide?" asked the girl.

"Don't you know?"

"No, sir."

"Then your grandfather doesn't wish you to know. I am his lawyer—at least I am one of his lawyers—and a lawyer must respect the confidences of his clients."

Mary Louise looked at him wonderingly, for here was someone who evidently knew the entire truth.

"Do you believe my grandfather is a bad man?" she asked.

"No. I have the highest respect for Colonel Weatherby."

"Do you know his name to be Weatherby—or is it Hathaway?"

"I am his lawyer," reiterated Mr Conant.

"Is it possible that an innocent man would change his name and hide, rather than face an unjust accusation?"

"Yes."

Mary Louise sighed.

"I will go with you to the hotel and pay your bill," said the lawyer. "Then you may go to the house and talk to Hannah. When I have talked with her myself, we will determine what to do with you."

So they went to the hotel and the girl packed her suitcase and brought it downstairs.

"Queer!" said Mr Conant to her, fingering his locket. "Your bill has been paid by that man O'Gorman."

"How impertinent!" she exclaimed.

"There is also a note for you in your box."

The clerk handed her an envelope, which she opened. "I hope to be able to send you your grandfather's address very soon," wrote O'Gorman. "You will probably stay in Dorfield; perhaps with the Conants, with whom you lived before. You might try sending Colonel Weatherby a letter in care of Oscar Lawler, at Los Angeles, California. In any event, don't forget my card or neglect to wire me in case of emergency."

Having read this with considerable surprise the girl handed the note to Mr Conant, who slowly read it and gave a bark like that of an angry dog when he came to the name of the California attorney. Without remark he put the detective's letter in his pocket and picking up Mary Louise's suitcase led the girl outside to the street corner.

"This car will take you to within two blocks of my house," he said. "Can you manage your grip alone?"

"Easily," she assured him.

"You have carfare!"

"Yes, thank you."

"Then goodbye. I'll see you this evening."

He turned away and she boarded the street car.

XI

MARY LOUISE MEETS IRENE

As Mary Louise approached the home of the Conants, which was a pretty little house set far back in a garden filled with trees and shrubs, she was surprised to hear a joyous ragtime tune being drummed upon the piano—an instrument she remembered Mrs Conant kept in the house exclusively as an ornament, being unable to play it. Then, as the girl reached the porch, the melody suddenly stopped, a merry laugh rang out and a fresh, sweet voice was heard through the open window talking rapidly and with eager inflection.

"I wonder who that can be?" thought Mary Louise. Everyone had to speak loudly to poor Mrs Conant, who might be entertaining a visitor. She rang the bell and soon her old friend appeared in the doorway.

"My dear, dear child!" cried the good lady, recognizing the girl instantly and embracing her after a welcoming kiss. "Where on earth have you come from?"

"From Beverly," said Mary Louise with a smile, for in her depressed state of mind this warm greeting cheered her wonderfully.

"Come right in," said Mrs Conant, seizing the suitcase. "Have you had breakfast?"

MARY LOUISE MEETS IRENE

"Yes, indeed; hours ago. And I've seen Mr Conant at his office. He—he wanted me to talk to you."

She spoke loudly, as she had been accustomed to do, but now Mrs Conant wore on her ear an instrument similar in appearance to a small telephone receiver, and she seemed to hear quite distinctly through its mechanism. Indeed, she pointed to it with an air of pride and said: "I can hear a whisper, my dear!"

As Mary Louise was ushered into the cosy sitting room she looked for the piano-player and the owner of the merry laugh and cheery voice. Near the center of the room was a wheeled chair in which sat a young girl of about her own age—a rather pretty girl in spite of her thin frame and pallid countenance. She was neatly dressed in figured dimity, with a bright ribbon at her throat. A pair of expressive brown eyes regarded Mary Louise with questioning earnestness. Over her lap lay a coverlet; her slender white fingers rested upon the broad arms of her chair.

"This," said Mrs Conant, "is my niece, Irene Macfarlane, who is living with us just now and is the life and joy of our formerly dull household. You'll have to love her, Mary Louise, because no one can help doing so."

Mary Louise advanced to the chair and took one of the wan hands in her own. A thrill of pity flooded her heart for the unfortunate girl, who instantly noted her expression and met it with a charmingly spontaneous smile.

"Don't you dare think of me as a cripple!" she said warningly. "I am not at all helpless and my really-truly friends quickly forget this ugly wheeled chair. We're to be friends, are we not? And you're going to stay, because I see your baggage. Also I know all about you, Mary Louise Burrows, for Aunt Hannah never tires of singing your praises."

This was said so naturally and with such absence of affectation that Mary Louise could not fail to respond to the words and smile.

"I'm glad to find you here, Irene," she said, "and I don't know yet whether I'm to stay or not. That will depend on Mrs Conant's decision."

"Then you're to stay," promptly decided the hospitable lady, who by turning her mechanical ear toward the speaker seemed able to hear her words clearly.

"But you don't know all the complications yet," confessed the girl. "I've run away from school and—and there are other things you must know before you decide. Mr Conant wasn't at all enthusiastic over my coming here, I assure you, so I must tell you frankly the whole story of my adventures."

"Very good," returned Mrs Conant. "I think I can guess at most of the story, but you shall tell it in your own way. Presently Irene is going out to inspect the roses; she does that every morning; so when she is out of the way we'll have a nice talk together."

"I'm going now," said Irene, with a bright laugh at her dismissal. "Mary Louise won't be happy till everything is properly settled; nor will I, for I'm anxious to get acquainted with my new friend. So here I go and when you've had your talk out just whistle for me, Mary Louise."

She could propel the chair by means of rims attached to the wheels and, even as she spoke, began to roll herself out of the room. Mary Louise sprang to assist her, but the girl waved her away with a little laugh.

"I'm an expert traveler," she said, "and everyone lets me go and come as I please. Indeed, I'm very independent, Mary Louise, as you will presently discover."

Away she went, through the hall, out at the front door and along the broad porch, and when she had gone Mary Louise whispered softly into Mrs Conant's mechanical eardrum:

"What is wrong with her?"

"A good many things," was the reply, "although the brave child makes light of them all. One leg is badly withered and the foot of the other is twisted out of shape. She can stand on that foot to dress herself—which she insists on doing unaided—but she cannot walk a step. Irene has suffered a great deal, I think, and she's a frail little body; but she has the sweetest temperament in the world and seems happy and content from morn till night."

"It's wonderful!" exclaimed Mary Louise. "What caused her affliction?"

"It is the result of an illness she had when a baby. Irene is sixteen and has never known what it is to be well and strong, yet she never resents her fate, but says she is grateful for the blessings she enjoys. Her father died long ago and her mother about a year since; so, the child being an orphan, Peter and I have taken her to live with us."

"That is very kind of you," asserted Mary Louise with conviction.

"No; I fear it is pure selfishness," returned the good woman, "for until she came to us the old home had been dreadfully dull—the result, my dear, of your going away. And now tell me your story, and all about yourself, for I'm anxious to hear what brought you to Dorfield."

Mary Louise drew a chair close to that of Aunt Hannah Conant and confided to her all the worries and tribulations that had induced her to quit Miss Stearne's school and seek shelter with her old friends the Conants. Also, she related the episode of Detective O'Gorman and how she had first learned through him that her grandfather and her mother were not living in Dorfield.

"I'm dreadfully worried over Gran'pa Jim," said she, "for those terrible agents of the Secret Service seem bent on catching him. And he doesn't wish to be caught. If they arrested him, do you think they would put him in jail, Aunt Hannah?"

"I fear so," was the reply.

"What do they imagine he has done that is wrong?"

"I do not know," said Mrs Conant. "Peter never tells me anything about the private affairs of his clients, and I never ask him. But of one thing I am sure, my dear, and that is that Peter Conant would not act as Colonel Weatherby's lawyer, and try to shield him, unless he believed him innocent of any crime. Peter is a little odd, in some ways, but he's honest to the backbone."

"I know it," declared Mary Louise. "Also I know that Gran'pa Jim is a good man. Cannot the law make a mistake, Aunt Hannah?"

"It surely can, or there would be no use for lawyers. But do not worry over your grandfather, my child, for he seems quite able to take care of himself. It is nine or ten years since he became a fugitive—also making a fugitive of your poor mother, who would not desert him—and to this day the officers of the law have been unable to apprehend him. Be patient, dear girl, and accept the situation as you find it. You shall live with us until your people again send for you. We have excellent schools in Dorfield, where you will not be taunted with your grandfather's misfortunes because no one here knows anything about them."

"Doesn't Irene know?" asked Mary Louise.

"She only knows that your people are great travelers and frequently leave you behind them as they flit from place to place. She knows that you lived with us for three years and that we love you."

The girl became thoughtful for a time. "I can't understand," she finally said, "why Gran'pa Jim acts the way he does. Often he has told me, when I deserved censure, to 'face the music' and have it over with. Once he said that those who sin must suffer the penalty, because it is the law of both God and man, and he who seeks to escape a just penalty is a coward. Gran'pa knows he is innocent, but the government thinks he is guilty; so why doesn't he face the music and prove his innocence, instead of running away as a coward might do and so allow his good name to suffer reproach?"

Mrs Conant shook her head as if perplexed.

"That very question has often puzzled me, as it has you," she confessed. "Once I asked Peter about it and he scowled and said it might be just as well to allow Colonel Weatherby to mind his own business. The Colonel seems to have a good deal of money, and perhaps he fears that if he surrendered to the law it would be taken away from him, leaving you and your mother destitute."

"We wouldn't mind that," said the girl, "if Gran'pa's name could be cleared."

"After all," continued Mrs Conant reflectively, "I don't believe the Colonel is accused of stealing money, for Peter says his family is one of the oldest and richest in New York. Your grandfather inherited a vast fortune and added largely to it. Peter says he was an important man of affairs before this misfortune—whatever it was—overtook him."

"I can just remember our home in New York," said Mary Louise, also musingly, "for I was very young at the time. It was a beautiful big place, with a good many servants. I wonder what drove us from it?"

"Do you remember your father?" asked Mrs Conant.

"Not at all."

"Peter once told me he was a foreigner who fell desperately in love with your mother and married her without your grandfather's full approval. I believe Mr Burrows was a man of much political influence, for he served in the Department of State and had a good many admirers. Peter never knew why your grandfather opposed the marriage, for afterward he took Mr and Mrs Burrows to live with him and they were all good friends up to the day of your father's death. But this is ancient history and speculation on subjects we do not understand is sure to prove unsatisfactory. I wouldn't worry over your grandfather's troubles, my dear. Try to forget them."

"Grandfather's real name isn't Weatherby," said the girl. "It is Hathaway."

Mrs Conant gave a start of surprise.

"How did you learn that?" she asked sharply.

The girl took out her watch, pried open the back ease with a penknife and allowed Mrs Conant to read the inscription. Also she curiously watched the woman's face and noted its quick flush and its uneasy expression. Did the lawyer's wife know more than she had admitted?

If so, why was everyone trying to keep her in the dark?

"I cannot see that this helps to solve the mystery," said Mrs Conant in a brisk tone as she recovered from her surprise. "Let us put the whole thing out of mind, Mary Louise, or it will keep us all stirred up and in a muddle of doubt. I shall tell Peter you are to live with us, and your old little room at the back of the hall is all ready for you. Irene has the next room, so you will be quite neighborly. Go and put away your things and then we'll whistle for Irene."

Mary Louise went to the well-remembered room and slowly and thoughtfully unpacked her suitcase. She was glad to find a home again among congenial people, but she was growing more and more perplexed over the astonishing case of Gran'pa Jim. It worried her to find that an occasional doubt would cross her mind in spite of her intense loyalty to her dearly loved grandparent. She would promptly drive out the doubt, but it would insist on intruding again.

"Something is wrong somewhere," she sighed. "There must be some snarl that even Gran'pa Jim can't untangle; and, if he can't, I'm sure no one else can. I wish I could find him and that he would tell me all about it. I suppose he thinks I'm too young to confide in, but I'm almost sixteen now and surely that's old enough to understand things. There were girls at school twenty years old that I'm sure couldn't reason as well as I can."

After a while she went downstairs and joined Irene in the garden, where the chair-girl was trimming rose bushes with a

MARY LOUISE MEETS IRENE

pair of stout scissors. She greeted Mary Louise with her bright smile, saying:

"I suppose everything is fixed up, now, and we can begin to get acquainted."

"Why, we ARE acquainted," declared Mary Louise. "Until today I had never heard of you, yet it seems as if I had known you always."

"Thank you," laughed Irene; "that is a very pretty compliment, I well realize. You have decided to stay, then?"

"Aunt Hannah has decided so, but Mr Conant may object."

"He won't do that," was the quick reply. "Uncle Peter may be an autocrat in his office, but I've noticed that Aunt Hannah is the ruler of this household."

Mr Conant may have noticed that, also, for he seemed not at all surprised when his wife said she had decided to keep Mary Louise with them. But after the girls had gone to bed that night the lawyer had a long talk with his better half, and thereafter Mary Louise's presence was accepted as a matter of course. But Mr Conant said to her the next morning:

"I have notified your grandfather, at his six different addresses, of your coming to us, so I ought to receive his instructions within the next few days. Also, today I will write Miss Stearne that you are here and why you came away from the school."

"Will you ask her to send my trunk?"

"Not now. We will first await advices from Colonel Weatherby."

These "advices" were received three days later in the form of a brief telegram from a Los Angeles attorney. The message read: "Colonel Weatherby requests you to keep M. L. in Dorfield until further instructions. Money forwarded. Hot. Caution." It was signed "O. L." and when Mr Conant showed Mary Louise the message she exclaimed:

"Then Mr O'Gorman was right!"

"In what way?" questioned the lawyer.

"In the note he left for me at the hotel he said I might find my grandfather by writing to Oscar Lawler at Los Angeles, California. This telegram is from Los Angeles and it is signed 'O. L.' which must mean 'Oscar Lawler.'"

"How clever!" said Mr Conant sarcastically.

"That proves, of course, that Gran'pa Jim and mother are in California. But how did the detective know that?" she asked wonderingly.

"He didn't know it," answered Peter Conant. "On the contrary, this message proves to me that they are not there at all."

"But the telegram says—"

"Otherwise," continued the lawyer, "the telegram would not have come from that far-away point on the Pacific coast. There now remain five other places where Colonel Weatherby might be located. The chances are, however, that he is not in any of them."

Mary Louise was puzzled. It was altogether too bewildering for her comprehension.

"Here are two strange words," said she, eyeing the telegram she still held. "What does 'hot' mean, Mr Conant?"

"It means," he replied, "that the government spies are again seeking Colonel Weatherby. The word 'caution' means that we must all take care not to let any information escape us that might lead to his arrest. Don't talk to strangers, Mary Louise; don't talk to anyone outside our family of your grandfather's affairs, or even of your own affairs. The safety of Colonel Weatherby depends, to a great extent, on our all being silent and discreet."

XII

A CHEERFUL COMRADE

The more Mary Louise saw of Irene Macfarlane the more she learned to love her. No one could be miserable or despondent for long in the chair-girl's society, because she was always so bright and cheery herself. One forgot to pity her or even to deplore her misfortunes while listening to her merry chatter and frank laughter, for she seemed to find genuine joy and merriment in the simplest incidents of the life about her.

"God has been so good to me, Mary Louise!" she once exclaimed as they were sitting together in the garden. "He has given me sight, that I may revel in bookland and in the beauties of flowers and trees and shifting skies and the faces of my friends. He has given me the blessing of hearing, that I may enjoy the strains of sweet music and the songs of the birds and the voices of those I love. And I can scent the fragrance of the morning air, the perfume of the roses and—yes! even the beefsteak Aunt Hannah is frying for supper. The beefsteak tastes as good to me as it does to you. I can feel the softness of your cheek; I can sing melodies, in my own way, whenever my heart swells with joy. I can move about, by means of this wonderful chair, without the bother of walking. You don't envy me, Mary Louise, because you enjoy almost equal blessings; but you must admit I have reason for being happy."

Irene read a good many books and magazines and through the daily papers kept well posted on the world's affairs. Indeed, she was much better posted than Mary Louise, who, being more active, had less leisure to think and thus absorb the full meaning of all that came to her notice. Irene would play the piano for hours at a time, though obliged to lean forward in her chair to reach the keys, and her moods ran the gamut from severely classical themes to ragtime, seeming to enjoy all equally. She also sewed and mended with such consummate skill that Mary Louise, who was rather awkward with her needle, marveled at her talent.

Nor was this the end of the chair-girl's accomplishments, for Irene had a fancy for sketching and made numerous caricatures of those persons with whom she came in contact. These contained so much humor that Mary Louise was delighted with them—especially one of "Uncle Peter" toying with his watch fob and staring straight ahead of him with round, expressionless eyes.

"Really, Irene, I believe you could paint," she once said.

"No," answered her friend, "I would not be so wicked as to do that. All imitations of Nature seem to me a mock of God's handiwork, which no mortal brush can hope to equal. I shall never be so audacious, I hope. But a photograph is a pure reflex of Nature, and my caricatures, which are merely bits of harmless fun, furnish us now and then a spark of humor to make us laugh, and laughter is good for the soul. I often laugh at my own sketches, as you know. Sometimes I laugh at their whimsical conception, before ever I put pencil to paper. Lots of caricatures I make secretly, laughing over and then destroying them for fear they might be seen and hurt the feelings of their innocent subjects. Why, Mary Louise, I drew your doleful face only yesterday, and it was so funny I shrieked with glee. You heard me and looked over at me with a smile that made the caricature lie, so I promptly tore it up. It had served its purpose, you see."

So many of these quaint notions filled the head of the crippled girl that Mary Louise's wondering interest in her never flagged. It was easy to understand why Mrs Conant had declared that Irene was the joy and life of the household, for it was impossible to remain morbid or blue in her presence.

For this reason, as well as through the warm and sincere affection inspired by Irene, Mary Louise came by degrees to confide to her the entire story of the mystery that surrounded her grandfather and influenced the lives of her mother and herself. Of her personal anxieties and fears she told her new friend far more than she had ever confessed to anyone else and her disclosures were met by ready sympathy.

"Phoo!" cried Irene. "This isn't a REAL trouble; it will pass away. Everything passes away in time, Mary Louise, for life is a succession of changes—one thing after another. Remember the quotation: 'Whate'er may be thy fate today, remember—this will pass away.' I love that little saying and it has comforted me and given me courage many a time."

"Life will also pass away," observed Mary Louise pessimistically.

"To be sure. Isn't that a glad prospect? To pass to a new life, to new adventures, planned for us by the wisdom of God, is the most glorious promise we mortals possess. In good time that joy will be ours, but now we must make the most of our present blessings. I take it, Mary Louise, that there is a purpose in everything—a Divine Purpose, you know—and that those who most patiently accept their trials will have the better future recompense. What's a twisted ankle or a shriveled leg to do with happiness? Or even a persecuted grandfather? We're made of better stuff, you and I, than to cry at such babyish bumps. My! what a lot of things we both have to be thankful for."

Somehow these conversations cheered Mary Louise considerably and her face soon lost its drawn, worried look and became almost as placid as in the days when she had Gran'pa

Jim beside her and suspected no approaching calamity. Gran'pa Jim would surely have loved Irene, had he known her, because their ideas of life and duty were so similar.

As it was now less than a month to the long summer vacation, Mary Louise did not enter the Dorfield High School but studied a little at home, so as not to get "rusty," and passed most of her days in the society of Irene Macfarlane. It was a week or so after her arrival that Peter Conant said to her one evening:

"I have now received ample funds for all your needs, Mary Louise, so I have sent to Miss Stearne to have your trunk and books forwarded."

"Oh; then you have heard from Gran'pa Jim?" she asked eagerly.

"Yes."

"Where is he?"

"I do not know," chopping the words apart with emphasis. "The Colonel has been very liberal. I am to put twenty dollars in cash in your pocketbook and you are to come to me for any further sums you may require, which I am ordered to supply without question. I would have favored making you an allowance, had I been consulted, but the Colonel is—eh—eh—the Colonel is the Colonel."

"Didn't Gran'pa Jim send me any letter, or—any information at all?" she asked wistfully.

"Not a word."

"In my last letter, which you promised me to forward, I begged him to write me," she said, with disappointment.

Peter Conant made no reply. He merely stared at her. But afterward, when the two girls were alone, Irene said to her:

"I do not think you should beg your grandfather to write you. A letter might be traced by his enemies, you know, and that would mean his undoing. He surely loves you and bears you in mind, for he has provided for your comfort in every possible way. Even your letters to him may be dangerous, although they reach him in such roundabout ways. If I were you, Mary Louise, I'd accept the situation as I found it and not demand more than your grandfather and your mother are able to give you."

This frank advice Mary Louise accepted in good part and through the influence of the chair-girl she gradually developed a more contented frame of mind.

Irene was a persistent reader of books and one of Mary Louise's self-imposed duties was to go to the public library and select such volumes as her friend was likely to be interested in. These covered a wide range of subjects, although historical works and tales of the age of chivalry seemed to appeal to Irene more than any others. Sometimes she would read aloud, in her sweet, sympathetic voice, to Mary Louise and Mrs Conant, and under these conditions they frequently found themselves interested in books which, if read by themselves, they would be sure to find intolerably dry and uninteresting. The crippled girl had a way of giving more than she received and, instead of demanding attention, would often entertain the sound-limbed ones of her immediate circle.

XIII

BUB SUCCUMBS TO FORCE

One day Peter Conant abruptly left his office, came home and packed his grip and then hurried downtown and caught the five o'clock train for New York. He was glum and uncommunicative, as usual, merely telling Aunt Hannah that business called him away and he did not know when he would be back.

A week later Peter appeared at the family breakfast table, having arrived on the early morning express, and he seemed in a more gracious mood than usual. Indeed, he was really talkative.

"I met Will Morrison in New York, Hannah," he said to his wife. "He was just sailing for London with his family and will remain abroad all summer. He wanted us to occupy his mountain place, Hillcrest Lodge, during July and August, and although I told him we couldn't use the place he insisted on my taking an order on his man to turn the shack over to us."

"The shack!" cried Aunt Hannah indignantly. "Why, Peter, Hillcrest Lodge is a little palace. It is the cosiest, most delightful place I have ever visited. Why shouldn't we accept Will Morrison's proposition to occupy it?"

"I can't leave my business."

"You could run up every Friday afternoon, taking the train to Millbank and the stage to Hillcrest, and stay with us till Monday morning."

He stared at her reflectively.

"Would you be safe in that out-of-the-way place?" he asked.

"Of course. Didn't you say Will had a man for caretaker? And only a few scattered cottages are located near by, so we shall be quite by ourselves and wholly unmolested. I mean to go, and take the girls. The change will do us all good, so you may as well begin to make arrangements for the trip."

Peter Conant stared awhile and then resumed his breakfast without comment. Mary Louise thought she saw a smile flicker over his stolid features for a moment, but could not be positive. Aunt Hannah had spoken in a practical, matter-of-fact way that did not admit of argument.

"Let me see," she resumed; "we will plan to leave on Thursday morning, over the branch road, which will get us to Millbank by noon. If you telegraph the stage-driver to meet us we can reach Hillcrest Lodge by three o'clock—perhaps earlier—and that will enable us to get settled before dark. That is far better than taking the afternoon train. Will you make the proper arrangements, Peter?"

"Yes," he briefly replied.

As he was leaving the house after breakfast he fixed his stare on Irene and said to her:

"In New York I ran across a lot of second-hand books at an auction sale—old novels and romances which you will probably like. I bought the lot and shipped them home. If they arrive in time you can take them to Hillcrest and they will keep you reading all summer."

"Oh, thank you, Uncle Peter!" exclaimed the chair-girl gratefully.

"Have you any—any—news of Gran'pa Jim?" asked Mary Louise diffidently.

"No," he said and walked away.

During the few days that remained before their exodus they were busy preparing for the anticipated vacation. Summer gowns had to be looked over and such things gathered together as might be useful during their two months' stay at Hillcrest.

"Of course no one will see us," remarked Aunt Hannah; "it's really the jumping-off place of the world; but Will Morrison has made it as cosy as possible and we three, with just Peter at the week-ends, can amuse one another without getting lonely. Peter will fish in the mountain streams, of course, and that's the reason he is allowing us to go. We've visited the Morrisons two or three times at the Lodge and Peter has fished for trout every minute he was there."

"Who are the Morrisons?" asked Mary Louise.

"Will Morrison is a rich banker and his wife Sallie was an old schoolmate of mine. The Lodge is only a little resort of theirs, you know, for in the city they live in grand style. I know you girls will enjoy the place, for the scenery is delightful and the clear mountain air mighty invigorating."

All girls delight in change of location and although Irene was a little worried over the difficulties of getting to Hillcrest Lodge in her crippled condition, she was as eager to go as was Mary Louise. And she made the trip more comfortably than she had feared.

At Millbank the stage-driver fixed a comfortable seat for her in his carryall and loaded the boxes and baggage and the wheeled chair and the box of books—which had arrived from New York—on the railed top of his bus, and then they drove away through a rough but picturesque country that drew from the girls many exclamations of delight.

Presently they came to a small group of dwellings called the "Huddle," which lay at the foot of the mountain. Then up a winding path the four horses labored patiently, halting often to rest and get their breaths. At such times the passengers gloried in the superb views of the valley and its farms and were never impatient to proceed. They passed one or two modest villas, for this splendid location had long ago been discovered by a few others besides Will Morrison who loved to come here for their vacations and so escape the maddening crowds of the cities.

Aunt Hannah had planned the trip with remarkable accuracy, for at about three o'clock the lumbering stage stopped at a pretty chalet half hidden among the tall pines and overlooking a steep bluff. Here the baggage and boxes were speedily unloaded.

"I gottagit back ter meet the aft'noon train," said Bill Coombs, their driver. "They won't be any more passingers in this direction, tain't likely, 'cause the houses 'roun' here is mighty scattered an' no one's expectin' nobody, as I know of. But in the other direction from Millbank—Sodd Corners way—I may catch a load, if I'm lucky."

So back he drove, leaving the Conants' traps by the roadside, and Peter began looking around for Morrison's man. The doors of the house were fast locked, front and rear. There was no one in the barn or the shed-like garage, where a rusty looking automobile stood. Peter looked around the grounds in vain. Then he whistled. Afterward he began bawling out "Hi, there!" in a voice that echoed lonesomely throughout the mountain side.

And, at last, when they were all beginning to despair, a boy came slouching around a corner of the house, from whence no one could guess. He was whittling a stick and he continued to whittle while he stared at the unexpected arrivals and slowly advanced. When about fifteen paces away he halted, with feet planted well apart, and bent his gaze sturdily on his stick and knife. He was barefooted, dressed in faded blue-jeans overalls and a rusty gingham shirt—the two united by a strap over one shoulder—and his head was covered by a broad Scotch golf cap much too big for him and considerably too warm for the season.

"Come here!" commanded Mr Conant.

The boy did not move, therefore the lawyer advanced angrily toward him.

"Why didn't you obey me?" he asked.

"They's gals there. I hates gals," said the boy in a confidential tone. "Any sort o' men critters I kin stand, but gals gits my goat."

"Who are you?" inquired Mr Conant.

"Me? I'm jus' Bub."

"Where is Mr Morrison's man?"

"Meanin' Talbot? Gone up to Mark's Peak, to guide a gang o' hunters f'm the city."

"When did he go?" asked the lawyer.

"I guess a Tuesday. No—a Wednesday."

"And when will he be back?"

The boy whittled, abstractedly.

"Answer me!"

"How kin I? D'ye know where Mark's Peak is?"

"No."

"It takes a week tergitthar; they'll likely hunt two er three weeks; mebbe more; ye kin tell that as well as I kin. Mister Will's gone ter You-RUPP with Miss' Morrison, so Talbot he won't be in no hurry ter come back."

"Great Caesar! Here's a pretty mess. Are you Talbot's boy?"

"Nope. I'm a Grigger, an' live over in the holler, yonder."

"What are you doing here?"

"Earnin' two bits a week."

"How?"

"Lookin' after the place."

"Very well. Mr Morrison has given us permission to use the Lodge while he is away, so unlock the doors and help get the baggage in."

The boy notched the stick with his knife, using great care.

"Talbot didn't say nuth'n' 'bout that," he remarked composedly.

Mr Conant uttered an impatient ejaculation. It was one of his peculiarities to give a bark similar to that of a dog when greatly annoyed. After staring at the boy a while he took out Will Morrison's letter to Talbot, opened it and held it before Bub's face.

"Read that!" he cried.

Bub grinned and shook his head.

"*I* kain't read," he said.

Mr Conant, in a loud and severe voice, read Mr Morrison's instruction to his man Talbot to do everything in his power to make the Conants comfortable and to serve them as faithfully as he did his own master. The boy listened, whittling slowly. Then he said:

"Mebbe that's all right; an' ag'in, mebbetain't. Seein' as I kain't read I ain't goin' ter take no one's word fer it."

"You insolent brat!" exclaimed Peter Conant, highly incensed. Then he turned and called: "Come here, Mary Louise."

Mary Louise promptly advanced and with every step she made the boy retreated a like distance, until the lawyer seized his arm and held it in a firm grip.

"What do you mean by running away?" he demanded.

"I hates gals," retorted Bub sullenly.

"Don't be a fool. Come here, Mary Louise, and read this letter to the boy, word for word."

Mary Louise, marking the boy's bashfulness and trying to restrain a smile, read Mr Morrison's letter.

"You see," said the lawyer sharply, giving Bub a little shake, "those are the exact words of the letter. We're going to enter the Lodge and take possession of it, as Mr Morrison has told us to do, and if you don't obey my orders I shall give you a good flogging. Do you understand that?"

Bub nodded, more cheerfully.

"If ye do it by force," said he, "that lets me out. Nobody kin blame me if I'm forced."

Mary Louise laughed so heartily that the boy cast an upward, half-approving glance at her face. Even Mr Conant's stern visage relaxed.

"See here, Bub," he said, "obey my orders and no harm can come to you. This letter is genuine and if you serve us faithfully while we are here I'll—I'll give you four bits a week."

"Heh? Four bits!"

"Exactly. Four bits every week."

"Gee, that'll make six bits a week, with the two Talbot's goin' ter give me. I'm hanged ef I don't buy a sweater fer next winter, afore the cold weather comes!"

"Very good," said Mr Conant. "Now get busy and let us in."

Bub deliberately closed the knife and put it in his pocket, tossing away the stick.

"Gals," he remarked, with another half glance at Mary Louise, "ain't ter my likin'; but FOUR BITS—"

He turned and walked away to where a wild rosebush clambered over one corner of the Lodge. Pushing away the thick, thorny branches with care, he thrust in his hand and drew out a bunch of keys.

"If it's jus' the same t' you, sir, I'd ruther ye'd snatch 'em from my hand," he suggested. "Then, if I'm blamed, I kin prove a alibi."

Mr Conant was so irritated that he literally obeyed the boy's request and snatched the keys. Then he led the way to the front door.

"It's that thin, brass one," Bub hinted.

Mr Conant opened the front door. The place was apparently in perfect order.

"Go and get Hannah and Irene, please," said Peter to Mary Louise, and soon they had all taken possession of the cosy

Lodge, had opened the windows and aired it and selected their various bedrooms.

"It is simply delightful!" exclaimed Irene, who was again seated in her wheeled chair, "and, if Uncle Peter will build a little runway from the porch to the ground, as he did at home, I shall be able to go and come as I please."

Meantime Aunt Hannah—as even Mary Louise now called Mrs Conant—ransacked the kitchen and cupboards to discover what supplies were in the house. There was a huge stock of canned goods, which Will Morrison had begged them to use freely, and the Conants had brought a big box of other groceries with them, which was speedily unpacked.

While the others were thus engaged in settling and arranging the house, Irene wheeled her chair to the porch, on the steps of which sat Bub, again whittling. He had shown much interest in the crippled girl, whose misfortune seemed instantly to dispel his aversion for her sex, at least so far as she was concerned. He was not reluctant even to look at her face and he watched with astonishment the ease with which she managed her chair. Having overheard, although at a distance, most of the boy's former conversation with Uncle Peter, Irene now began questioning him.

"Have you been eating and sleeping here?"

"Of course," answered Bub.

"In the Lodge?"

"No; over in Talbot's house. That's over the ridge, yonder; it's only a step, but ye kain't see it f'm here. My home's in the South Holler, four mile away."

"Do you cook your own meals?"

"Nobudy else ter do it."

"And don't you get dreadfully lonesome at night?"

"Who? Me? Guess not. What the Sam Hill is they to be lonesome over?"

"There are no near neighbors, are there?"

"Plenty. The Barker house is two mile one way an' the Bigbee house is jus' half a mile down the slope; guess ye passed it, comin' up; but they ain't no one in the Bigbee house jus' now, 'cause Bigbee got shot on the mount'n las' year, a deer hunt'n', an' Bigbee's wife's married another man what says he's delicate like an' can't leave the city. But neighbors is plenty. Six mile along the canyon lives Doolittle."

Irene was delighted with Bub's quaint language and ways and before Mrs Conant called her family to the simple improvised dinner the chair-girl had won the boy's heart and already they were firm friends.

XIV

A CALL FROM AGATHA LORD

Hillcrest Lodge was perched upon a broad shelf of the wooded mountain, considerably nearer to the bottom than to the top, yet a stiff climb from the plain below. Behind it was a steep cliff; in front there was a gradual descent covered with scrub but affording a splendid view of the lowlands. At one side was the rocky canyon with its brook struggling among the boulders, and on the other side the roadway that wound up the mountain in zigzag fashion, selecting the course of least resistance.

Will Morrison was doubtless a mighty hunter and an expert fisherman, for the "den" at the rear of the Lodge was a regular museum of trophies of the chase. Stag and doe heads, enormous trout mounted on boards, antlers of wild mountain sheep, rods, guns, revolvers and hunting-knives fairly lined the wails, while a cabinet contained reels, books of flies, cartridge belts, creels and many similar articles. On the floor were rugs of bear, deer and beaver. A shelf was filled with books on sporting subjects. There was a glass door that led onto a little porch at the rear of the Lodge and a big window that faced the cliff.

This sanctum of the owner rather awed the girls when first they examined it, but they found it the most fascinating place in all the house and Irene was delighted to be awarded the bedroom that adjoined it. The other bedrooms were on the upper floor.

"However," said Mr Conant to Irene, "I shall reserve the privilege of smoking my evening pipe in this den, for here is a student lamp, a low table and the easiest chairs in all the place. If you keep your bedroom door shut you won't mind the fumes of tobacco."

"I don't mind them anyhow, Uncle Peter," she replied.

Bub Grigger helped get in the trunks and boxes. He also filled the woodbox in the big living room and carried water from the brook for Aunt Hannah, but otherwise he was of little use to them. His favorite occupation was whittling and he would sit for hours on one of the broad benches overlooking the valley, aimlessly cutting chips from a stick without forming it into any object whatsoever.

"I suppose all this time he is deeply thinking," said Mary Louise as the girls sat on the porch watching him, the day after their arrival, "but it would be interesting to know what direction Bub's thoughts take."

"He must be figuring up his earnings and deciding how long it will take to buy that winter sweater," laughed Irene. "I've had a bit of conversation with the boy already and his ideas struck me as rather crude and undeveloped."

"One idea, however, is firmly fixed in his mind," declared Mary Louise. "He 'hates gals.'"

"We must try to dispel that notion. Perhaps he has a big sister at home who pounds him, and therefore he believes all girls are alike."

"Then let us go to him and make friends," suggested Mary Louise. "If we are gentle with the boy we may win him over."

Mr Conant had already made a runway for the chair, so they left the porch and approached Bub, who saw them coming and slipped into the scrub, where he speedily disappeared from view. At other times, also, he shyly avoided the girls, until they

A CALL FROM AGATHA LORD

began to fear it would be more difficult to "make friends" than they had supposed.

Monday morning Mr Conant went down the mountain road, valise in hand, and met Bill Coombs the stage-driver at the foot of the descent, having made this arrangement to save time and expense. Peter had passed most of his two days' vacation in fishing and had been so successful that he promised Aunt Hannah he would surely return the following Friday. He had instructed Bub to "take good care of the womenfolks" during his absence, but no thought of danger occurred to any of them. The Morrisons had occupied the Lodge for years and had never been molested in any way. It was a somewhat isolated place but the country people in the neighborhood were thoroughly honest and trustworthy.

"There isn't much for us to do here," said Mary Louise when the three were left alone, "except to read, to eat and to sleep—lazy occupations all. I climbed the mountain a little way yesterday, but the view from the Lodge is the best of all and if you leave the road you tear your dress to shreds in the scrub."

"Well, to read, to eat and to sleep is the very best way to enjoy a vacation," asserted Aunt Hannah. "Let us all take it easy and have a good time."

Irene's box of books which Mr Conant had purchased for her in New York had been placed in the den, where she could select the volumes as she chose, and the chair-girl found the titles so alluring that she promised herself many hours of enjoyment while delving among them. They were all old and second-hand—perhaps fourth-hand or fifth-hand—as the lawyer had stated, and the covers were many of them worn to tatters; but "books is books," said Irene cheerily, and she believed they would not prove the less interesting in contents because of their condition. Mostly they were old romances, historical essays and novels, with a sprinkling of fairy tales and books of verse—just the subjects Irene most loved.

"Being exiles, if not regular hermits," observed the crippled girl, sunning herself on the small porch outside the den, book in hand, "we may loaf and dream to our hearts' content, and without danger of reproach."

But not for long were they to remain wholly secluded. On Thursday afternoon they were surprised by a visitor, who suddenly appeared from among the trees that lined the roadway and approached the two girls who were occupying a bench at the edge of the bluff.

The new arrival was a lady of singularly striking appearance, beautiful and in the full flush of womanhood, being perhaps thirty years of age. She wore a smart walking-suit that fitted her rounded form perfectly, and a small hat with a single feather was jauntily perched upon her well-set head. Hair and eyes, almost black, contrasted finely with the bloom on her cheeks. In her ungloved hand she held a small walking-stick.

Advancing with grace and perfect self-possession, she smiled and nodded to the two young girls and then, as Mary Louise rose to greet her, she said:

"I am your nearest neighbor, and so I have climbed up here to get acquainted. I am Agatha Lord, but of course you do not know me, because I came from Boston, whereas you came from—from—"

"Dorfield," said Mary Louise. "Pray be seated. Let me present Irene Macfarlane; and I am Mary Louise Burrows. You are welcome, Miss Lord—or should I say Mrs Lord?"

"Miss is correct," replied their visitor with a pleasant laugh, which brought an answering smile to the other faces; "but you must not address me except as 'Agatha.' For here in the wilderness formalities seem ridiculous. Now let us have a cosy chat together."

"Won't you come into the Lodge and meet Mrs Conant?"

"Not just yet. You may imagine how that climb winded me, although they say it is only half a mile. I've taken the Bigbee house, just below you, you know, and I arrived there last night to get a good rest after a rather strenuous social career at home. Ever since Easter I've been on the 'go' every minute and I'm really worn to a frazzle."

She did not look it, thought Mary Louise. Indeed, she seemed the very picture of health.

"Ah," said she, fixing her eyes on Irene's book, "you are very fortunate. The one thing I forgot to bring with me was a supply of books, and there is not a volume—not even a prayer-book—in the Bigbee house. I shall go mad in these solitudes if I cannot read."

"You may use my library," promised Irene, sympathizing with Miss Lord's desire. "Uncle Peter brought a great box of books for me to read and you are welcome to share their delights with me, I believe there are fifty of them, at the least; but many were published ages ago and perhaps," with a glance at the dainty hands, "you won't care to handle second-hand books."

"This ozonic air will fumigate them," said Agatha Lord carelessly. "We don't absorb bindings, Irene, but merely the thoughts of the authors. Books are the one banquet-table whereat we may feast without destroying the delicacy or flavor of the dishes presented. As long as the pages hold together and the type is legible a book is as good as when new."

"I like pretty bindings, though," declared Irene, "for they dress pretty thoughts in fitting attire. An ill-looking book, whatever its contents, resembles the ugly girl whose only redeeming feature is her good heart. To be beautiful without and within must have been the desire of God in all things."

Agatha gave her a quick look of comprehension. There was an unconsciously wistful tone in the girl's voice. Her face, though pallid, was lovely to view; her dress was dainty and arranged with care; she earnestly sought to be as beautiful "without and within" as was possible, yet the twisted limbs forbade her attaining the perfection she craved.

They sat together for an hour in desultory conversation and Agatha Lord certainly interested the two younger girls very much. She was decidedly worldly in much of her gossip but quick to perceive when she infringed the susceptibilities of her less sophisticated companions and was able to turn the subject cleverly to more agreeable channels.

"I've brought my automobile with me," she said, "and, unless you have a car of your own, we will take some rides through the valley together. I mean to drive to Millbank every day for mail."

"There's a car here, which belongs to Mr Morrison," replied Mary Louise, "but as none of us understands driving it we will gladly accept your invitations to ride. Do you drive your own car?"

"Yes, indeed; that is the joy of motoring; and I care for my car, too, because the hired chauffeurs are so stupid. I didn't wish the bother of servants while taking my 'rest cure,' and so my maid and I are all alone at the Bigbee place."

After a time they went into the house, where Miss Lord was presented to Aunt Hannah, who welcomed their neighbor with her accustomed cordiality. In the den Agatha pounced upon the books and quickly selected two which she begged permission to take home with her.

"This is really a well selected collection," she remarked, eyeing the titles critically. "Where did Mr Conant find it?"

"At an auction of second-hand junk in New York," explained Irene. "Uncle Peter knows that I love the old-fashioned books best but I'm sure he didn't realize what a good collection this is."

As she spoke, Irene was listlessly running through the leaves of two or three volumes she had not before examined, when in one of them her eye was caught by a yellowed sheet of correspondence paper, tucked among the pages at about midway between the covers. Without removing the sheet she leaned over to examine the fine characters written upon it and presently exclaimed in wondering tones:

"Why, Mary Louise! Here is an old letter about your mother—yes, and here's something about your grandfather, too. How strange that it should be—"

"Let me see it!" cried Mary Louise, eagerly stretching out her hands.

But over her friend's shoulder Irene caught the expression of Agatha Lord—tense, startled, with a gleam of triumph in the dark eyes. It frightened her, that look on the face of one she had deemed a stranger, and it warned her. She closed the book with a little slam of decision and tucked it beside her in her chair.

"No," she said positively, "no one shall see the letter until I've had time to read it myself."

"But what was it about?" asked Mary Louise.

"I don't know, yet; and you're not to ask questions until I DO know," retorted Irene, calmly returning Miss Lord's curious gaze while addressing Mary Louise. "These are my books, you must admit, and so whatever I find in them belongs to me."

"Quite right, my dear," approved Agatha Lord, with her light, easy laugh. She knew that Irene had surprised her unguarded expression and wished to counteract the impression it had caused.

Irene returned the laugh with one equally insincere, saying to her guest:

"Help yourself to whatever books you like, neighbor. Carry them home, read them and return them at your convenience."

"You are exceedingly kind," answered Agatha and resumed her examination of the titles. Mary Louise had not observed the tell-tale expression on Miss Lord's face but she was shrewd enough to detect an undercurrent of ice in the polite phrases passing between her companions. She was consumed with curiosity to know more of the letter which Irene had found in the book but did not again refer to it in the presence of their visitor.

It was not long before Agatha rose to go, a couple of books tucked beneath her arm.

"Will you ride with me to Millbank tomorrow?" she asked, glancing from one face to another.

Mary Louise looked at Irene and Irene hesitated.

"I am not very comfortable without my chair," she said.

"You shall have the rear seat all to yourself, and it is big and broad and comfortable. Mary Louise will ride with me in front. I can easily drive the car up here and load you in at this very porch. Please come!"

"Very well, since you are so kind," Irene decided, and after a few more kindly remarks the beautiful Miss Lord left them and walked with graceful, swinging stride down the path to the road and down the road toward the Bigbee house.

XV

BUB'S HOBBY

When their visitor had departed Mary Louise turned to her friend.

"Now, Irene, tell me about that queer letter," she begged.

"Not yet, dear. I'm sure it isn't important, though it's curious to find such an old letter tucked away in a book Uncle Peter bought at an auction in New York—a letter that refers to your own people, in days long gone by. In fact, Mary Louise, it was written so long ago that it cannot possibly interest us except as proof of the saying that the world's a mighty small place. When I have nothing else to do I mean to read that old epistle from start to finish; then, if it contains anything you'd care to see, I'll let you have a look at it."

With this promise Mary Louise was forced to be content, for she did not wish to annoy Irene by further pleadings. It really seemed, on reflection, that the letter could be of little consequence to anyone. So she put it out of mind, especially as just now they spied Bub sitting on the bench and whittling as industriously as ever.

"Let me go to him first," suggested Irene, with a mischievous smile. "He doesn't seem at all afraid of me, for some reason, and after I've led him into conversation you can join us."

So she wheeled her chair over to where the boy sat. He glanced toward her as she approached the bench but made no movement to flee.

"We've had a visitor," said the girl, confidentially; "a lady who has taken the Bigbee house for the summer."

Bub nodded, still whittling.

"I know; I seen her drive her car up the grade on high," he remarked, feeling the edge of his knife-blade reflectively. "Seems like a real sport—fer a gal—don't she?"

"She isn't a girl; she's a grown woman."

"To me," said Bub, "ev'rything in skirts is gals. The older they gits, the more ornery, to my mind. Never seen a gal yit what's wuth havin' 'round."

"Some day," said Irene with a smile, "you may change your mind about girls."

"An' ag'in," said Bub, "I mayn't. Dad says he were soft in the head when he took up with marm, an' Talbot owned a wife once what tried ter pizen him; so he giv 'er the shake an' come here to live in peace; but Dad's so used to scoldin's thet he can't sleep sound in the open any more onless he lays down beside the brook where it's noisiest. Then it reminds him o' marm an' he feels like he's to home. Gals think they got the men scared, an' sometimes they guess right. Even Miss' Morrison makes Will toe the mark, an' Miss' Morrison ain't no slouch, fer a gal."

This somewhat voluble screed was delivered slowly, interspersed with periods of aimless whittling, and when Irene had patiently heard it through she decided it wise to change the subject.

"Tomorrow we are going to ride in Miss Lord's automobile," she remarked.

Bub grunted.

"She says she can easily run it up to our door. Do you believe that!"

"Why not?" he inquired. "Don't Will Morrison have a car? It's over there in the shed now."

"Could it be used?" quietly asked Mary Louise, who had now strolled up behind the bench unperceived.

Bub turned a scowling face to her, but she was looking out across the bluff. And she had broached a subject in which the boy was intensely interested.

"Thetthar car in there is a reg'lar hummer," he asserted, waving the knife in one hand and the stick in the other by way of emphasis. "Tain't much fer looks, ye know, but looks cuts no figger with machinery, s'long's it's well greased. On a hill, thet car's a cat; on a level stretch, she's a jack-rabbit. I've seen Will Morrison take 'er ter Millbank an' back in a hour—jus' one lonesome hour!"

"That must have been in its good days," observed Mary Louise. "The thing hasn't any tires on it now."

"Will takes the tires off ev'ry year, when he goes away, an' puts 'em in the cellar," explained Bub. "They's seven good tires down cellar now; I counted 'em the day afore ye come here."

"In that case," said Mary Louise, "if any of us knew how to drive we could use the car."

"Drive?" said Bub scornfully. "That's nuth'n'."

"Oh. Do you know how?"

"Me? I kin drive any car thet's on wheels. Two years ago, afore Talbot come, I used ter drive Will Morrison over t' Millbank ev'ry week t' catch the train; an' brung the car home ag'in; an' went fer Will when he come back."

"You must have been very young, two years ago," said Irene.

"Shucks. I'm goin' on fifteen this very minnit. When I were 'leven I druv the Higgins car fer 'em an' never hit the ditch once. Young! Wha'd'ye think I am—a KID?"

So indignant had he become that he suddenly rose and slouched away, nor could they persuade him to return.

"We're going to have a lot of fun with that boy, once we learn how to handle him," predicted Irene, when the two girls had enjoyed a good laugh at Bub's expense. "He seems a queer mixture of simplicity and shrewdness."

The next day Agatha Lord appeared in her big touring car and after lifting Irene in and making her quite comfortable on the back seat they rolled gayly away to Millbank, where they had lunch at the primitive restaurant, visited the post-office in the grocery store and amused themselves until the train came in and brought Peter Conant, who was loaded down with various parcels of merchandise Aunt Hannah had ordered.

The lawyer was greatly pleased to find a car waiting to carry him to the Lodge and after being introduced to Miss Lord, whose loveliness he could not fail to admire, he rode back with her in the front seat and left Mary Louise to sit inside with Irene and the packages. Bill Coombs didn't approve of this method of ruining his stage business and scowled at the glittering auto as it sped away across the plain to the mountain.

On this day Miss Lord proved an exceedingly agreeable companion to them all, even Irene forgetting for the time the strange expression she had surprised on Agatha's face at the time she found the letter. Mary Louise seemed to have quite forgotten that letter, for she did not again refer to it; but Irene, who had studied it closely in the seclusion of her own room that very night, had it rather persistently in mind and her eyes took on an added expression of grave and gentle commiseration whenever she looked at Mary Louise's unconscious face.

"It is much more fun," observed Peter Conant at breakfast the nest morning, "to ride to and from the station in a motor car than to patronize Bill Coombs' rickety, slow-going omnibus. But I can't expect our fair neighbor to run a stage line for my express accommodation."

"Will Morrison's motor car is here in the shed," said Mary Louise, and then she told of their conversation with Bub concerning it. "He says he has driven a car ever since he was eleven years old," she added.

"I wondered what that boy was good for," asserted the lawyer, "yet the very last thing I would have accused him of is being a chauffeur."

"Why don't you put on the tires and use the car?" asked Aunt Hannah.

"H-m. Morrison didn't mention the car to me. I suppose he forgot it. But I'm sure he'd be glad to have us use it. I'll talk with the boy."

Bub was found near the Talbot cottage in the gully. When Mr Conant and Mary Louise approached him, soon after finishing their breakfast, he was — as usual — diligently whittling.

"They tell me you understand running Mr Morrison's car," began the lawyer.

Bub raised his eyes a moment to the speaker's face but deemed an answer unnecessary.

"Is that true?" with an impatient inflection.

"Kin run any car," said Bub.

"Very well. Show me where the tires are and we will put them on. I want you to drive me to and from Millbank, hereafter."

Bub retained his seat and whittled.

"Hev ye got a order from Will Morrison, in writin'?" he demanded.

"No, but he will be glad to have me use the machine. He said everything at the Lodge was at my disposal."

"Cars," said Bub, "ain't like other things. A feller'll lend his huntin'-dog, er his knife, er his overcoat; but he's all-fired shy o' lendin' his car. Ef I runned it for ye, Will might blame ME."

Mr Conant fixed his dull stare on the boy's face, but Bub went on whittling. However, in the boy's inmost heart was a keen desire to run that motor car, as had been proposed. So he casually remarked:

"Ef ye forced me, ye know, I'd jus' hev to do it. Even Will couldn't blame me ef I were forced."

Mr Conant was so exasperated that the hint was enough. He seized the boy's collar, lifted him off the stump and kicked him repeatedly as he propelled his victim toward the house.

"Oh, Uncle Peter!" cried Mary Louise, distressed; but Peter was obdurate and Bub never whimpered. He even managed to close his knife, between kicks, and slip it into his trousers pocket.

When they came to the garage the lawyer halted, more winded than Bub, and demanded sharply:

"What is needed to put the car in shape to run?"

"Tires, gas'line, oil 'n' water."

"The tires are in the cellar, you say? Get them out or I'll skin you alive."

Bub nodded, grinning.

"Forcin' of me, afore a witness, lets me out," he remarked, cheerfully, and straightway went for the tires.

Irene wheeled herself out and joined Uncle Peter and Mary Louise in watching the boy attach the tires, which were on demountable rims and soon put in place. All were surprised at Bub's sudden exhibition of energy and his deft movements, for he worked with the assurance of a skilled mechanic.

"Now, we need gasoline," said Mr Conant. "I must order that from Millbank, I suppose."

"Onless ye want to rob Will Morrison's tank," agreed Bub.

"Oh; has he a tank of gasoline here?"

Bub nodded.

"A undergroun' steel tank. I dunno how much gas is in it, but ef ye forced me I'd hev to measure it."

Peter picked up a stick and shook it threateningly, whereat Bub smiled and walked to the rear of the garage where an iron plug appeared just above the surface of the ground. This he unscrewed with a wrench, thrust in a rod and drew it out again.

"'Bout forty gallon," he announced. "Thet's 'nough fer a starter, I guess."

"Then put some of it into the machine. Is there any oil?"

"Plenty oil."

Half an hour later Bub started the engine and rolled the car slowly out of its shed to the graveled drive in the backyard.

"All right, mister," he announced with satisfaction. "I dunno what Will'll say to this, but I kin prove I were forced. Want to take a ride now?"

"No," replied Mr Conant, "I merely wanted to get the car in shape. You are to take me to the station on Monday morning. Under the circumstances we will not use Morrison's car for pleasure rides, but only for convenience in getting from here to the trains and back. He surely cannot object to that."

Bub seemed disappointed by this decision. He ran the car around the yard two or three times, testing its condition, and then returned it to its shed. Mr Conant got his rod and reel and departed on a fishing excursion.

XVI

THE STOLEN BOOK

Miss Lord came up to the Lodge that Saturday forenoon and proved so agreeable to Aunt Hannah and the girls that she was invited to stay to lunch. Mr Conant was not present, for he had put a couple of sandwiches in his pocket and would not return home until dinner-time.

After luncheon they were all seated together on the benches at the edge of the bluff, which had become their favorite resort because the view was so wonderful. Mary Louise was doing a bit of fancy work, Irene was reading and Aunt Hannah, as she mended stockings, conversed in a desultory way with her guest.

"If you don't mind," said Agatha, after a time, "I'll run in and get me a book. This seems the place and the hour for dreaming, rather than gossip, and as we are all in a dreamy mood a good old-fashioned romance seems to me quite fitting for the occasion."

Taking permission for granted, she rose and sauntered toward the house. There was a serious and questioning look in Irene's eyes as they followed the graceful form of Miss Lord, but Mary Louise and Aunt Hannah paid no heed to their visitor's going in to select a book, it seemed so natural a thing for her to do.

It was fully fifteen minutes before Agatha returned, book in hand. Irene glanced at the title and gave a sigh of relief.

Without comment their guest resumed her seat and soon appeared to be immersed in her volume. Gradually the sun crossed the mountain and cast a black shadow over the plain below, a shadow which lengthened and advanced inch by inch until it shrouded the landscape spread beneath them.

"That is my sun-dial," remarked Mary Louise, dropping her needlework to watch the shifting scene. "When the shadow passes the Huddle, it's four o'clock; by the time it reaches that group of oaks, it is four-thirty; at five o'clock it touches the creek, and then I know it's time to help Aunt Hannah with the dinner."

Agatha laughed.

"Is it really so late?" she asked. "I see the shadow has nearly reached the brook."

"Oh! I didn't mean—"

"Of course not; but it's time I ran home, just the same. My maid Susan is a perfect tyrant and scolds me dreadfully if I'm late. May I take this book home, Irene? I'll return the others I have borrowed tomorrow."

"To be sure," answered Irene. "I'm rich in books, you know."

When Miss Lord went away the party broke up, for Aunt Hannah was already thinking of dinner and Mary Louise wanted to make one of Uncle Peter's favorite desserts. So Irene wheeled her chair into the house and entering the den began a sharp inspection of the place, having in mind exactly the way it had looked when last she left it. But presently she breathed a sigh of relief and went into her own room, for the den had not been disturbed. She wheeled herself to a small table in a corner of her chamber and one glance confirmed her suspicions.

For half an hour she sat quietly thinking, considering many things that might prove very important in the near future. The chair-girl knew little of life save what she had gleaned from books, but in some ways that was quite equal to personal experiences. At dinner she asked:

"Did you take a book from my room today, Mary Louise?"

"No," was the reply; "I have not been in your room since yesterday."

"Nor you, Aunt Hannah?"

"No, my dear. What book is missing?"

"It was entitled 'The Siberian Exile.'"

"Good gracious!" exclaimed Mary Louise. "Wasn't that the book you found the letter in?"

"Yes."

"And you say it is missing?"

"It has mysteriously disappeared."

"Nonsense," said Uncle Peter, who had returned with a fine string of trout. "No one would care to steal an old book, and the thing hasn't legs, you know."

"Nevertheless," said Irene gravely, "it is gone."

"And the letter with it!" added Mary Louise regretfully. "You ought to have let me read it while I could, Irene."

"What letter are you talking about?" asked the lawyer.

"It is nothing important, Uncle Peter," Irene assured him. "The loss of the book does not worry me at all."

Nor did it, for she knew the letter was not in it. And, to avoid further questioning on the part of Mr Conant, she managed to turn the conversation to less dangerous subjects.

XVII

THE HIRED GIRL

Mr Conant had just put on a comfortable smoking-jacket and slippers and seated himself in the den, pipe in mouth, when the old-fashioned knocker on the front door of the Lodge began to bang. It banged three times, so Mr Conant rose and made for the door.

Mrs Conant and Mary Louise were in the kitchen and Irene was in her own room. The lawyer reflected, with a deprecating glance at his unconventional costume, that their evening caller could be none other than their neighbor, the beautiful Miss Lord, so as he opened the door he regretted that his appearance was not more presentable.

But it was not Miss Lord who stood upon the porch awaiting admittance. It was a strange girl, who asked in a meek voice:

"Is this Hillcrest Lodge?"

"It is," replied the lawyer.

The girl came in without an invitation, bringing a carpet-bag in one hand and a bundle tied in a newspaper tucked under the other arm. As she stood in the lighted room she looked around inquiringly and said:

"I am Sarah Judd. Where is Mrs Morrison, please?"

Mr Conant stood and stared at her, his hands clasped behind his back in characteristic attitude. He could not remember ever having heard of Sarah Judd.

"Mrs Morrison," he said in his choppy voice, "is in Europe."

The girl stared at him in return, as if stupified. Then she sat down in the nearest chair and continued to stare. Finding her determined on silence, Mr Conant spoke again.

"The Morrisons are spending the summer abroad. I and my family are occupying the Lodge in their absence. I—eh—eh—I am Mr Conant, of Dorfield."

The girl sighed drearily. She was quite small, about seventeen years of age and dressed in a faded gingham over which she wore a black cloth coat that was rusty and frayed. A black straw hat, fearfully decorated with red velvet and mussed artificial flowers, was tipped over her forehead. Her features were not bad, but her nose was blotched, her face strongly freckled and her red hair very untidy. Only the mild blue eyes redeemed the unattractive face—eyes very like those of Mary Louise in expression, mused Mr Conant, as he critically eyed the girl.

"I have come here to work," she said after a long pause, during which she seemed trying to collect her thoughts. "I am Sarah Judd. Mrs Morrison said I must come here on Saturday, the tenth day of July, to go to work. This is the tenth day of July."

"H-m—h-m; I see. When did Mrs Morrison tell you that?"

"It was last September."

"Oh; so she hired you a year in advance and didn't tell you, afterward, that she was going abroad?"

"I didn't see her since, sir."

Mr Conant was perplexed. He went into the kitchen and told Aunt Hannah about it and the good woman came at once to interview Sarah Judd, followed by Mary Louise, who had just finished wiping the dishes.

"This seems very unfortunate for you," began Mrs Conant, regarding the strange girl with mild interest. "I suppose, when Mrs Morrison engaged you, she expected to pass the summer at the Lodge, and afterward she forgot to notify you."

Sarah Judd considered this soberly; then nodded her head.

"I've walked all the way from Millbank," she said with another sigh.

"Then you've had nothing to eat!" exclaimed Mary Louise, with ready sympathy. "May I get her something, Aunt Hannah?"

"Of course, my dear."

Both Mr and Mrs Conant felt rather embarrassed.

"I regret," said the latter, "that we do not need a maid at present. We do our own housework, you see."

"I have left a good place in Albany to come here," said Sarah, plaintively.

"You should have written to Mrs Morrison," declared the lawyer, "asking if she still required your services. Many unforeseen things may happen during a period of ten months."

"Mrs Morrison, she have paid me a month in advance," asserted the girl, in justification. "And she paid me my expenses to come here, too. She said I must not fail her; I should come to the Lodge on the tenth of July and do the work at the Lodge. She did not say she would be here. She did not say you would be here. She told me to come and work, and she paid me a month in advance, so I could give the money to my sister, who needed it then. And I must do as Mrs Morrison says. I am paid to work at the Lodge and so I must work at the Lodge. I cannot help that, can I?"

The lawyer was a man of experience, but this queer complication astonished him. He exchanged a questioning glance with his wife.

"In any event," said Mrs Conant, "the girl must stay here tonight, for it would be cruel to ask her to find her way down the mountain in the dark. We will put her in the maid's room, Peter, and tomorrow we can decide what to do with her."

"Very well," agreed Mr Conant and retreated to the den to have his smoke.

Mary Louise arranged some food on the kitchen table for Sarah Judd and after the girl had eaten, Mrs Conant took her to the maid's room, which was a very pleasant and well furnished apartment quite in keeping with all the comfortable appointments at Hillcrest Lodge, although it was built behind the kitchen and formed a little wing of its own.

Sarah Judd accepted these favors with meek resignation. Since her one long speech of explanation she had maintained silence. Leaving her in her room, the family congregated in the den, where Mr Conant was telling Irene about the queer arrival and the unfortunate misunderstanding that had occasioned it.

"The girl is not to blame," said Mary Louise. "She seems an honest little thing, resolved to do her duty. It is all Mrs Morrison's fault."

"Doesn't look like a very competent servant, either," observed Mr Conant, comfortably puffing his pipe.

"You can't tell that from appearances, Peter," replied Mrs Conant. "She can at least wash dishes and sweep and do the drudgery. Why not keep her?"

"Oh, my dear!"

"Mrs Morrison has paid her a month's wages, and Molly Morrison wouldn't have done that had not the girl been competent. It won't cost us anything to keep her—except her food—and it seems a shame to cast her adrift just because the Morrisons forgot to notify her they had changed their plans."

"Also," added Mary Louise, "Sarah Judd will be useful to us. This is Aunt Hannah's vacation, as well as a vacation for the rest of us, and a rest from cooking and housework would do her a heap of good."

"Looking at it from that viewpoint," said Peter, after puffing his pipe reflectively, "I approve of our keeping Sarah Judd. I believe it will please the Morrisons better than for us to send her away, and—it surely won't hurt Hannah to be a lady of leisure for a month or so."

XVIII

MARY LOUISE GROWS SUSPICIOUS

And so Sarah Judd's fate was decided. She prepared their Sunday morning breakfast and cooked it quite skillfully. Her appearance was now more tidy and she displayed greater energy than on the previous evening, when doubtless she was weary from her long walk. Mrs Conant was well pleased with the girl and found the relief from clearing the table and "doing" the dishes very welcome. Their Sunday dinner, which Sarah prepared unaided and served promptly at one o'clock, their usual hour, was a pleasant surprise to them all.

"The girl is a treasure," commented Mrs Conant, contentedly.

Sarah Judd was not talkative. When told she might stay she merely nodded her red head, displaying neither surprise nor satisfaction. Her eyes had a habit of roving continually from face to face and from object to object, yet they seemed to observe nothing clearly, so stolid was, their expression. Mary Louise tried to remember where she had noted a similar expression before, but could not locate it.

Miss Lord came over that afternoon and when told about the new maid and the manner of her appearance seemed a little startled and uneasy.

"I must see what she looks like," said she, "for she may prove a congenial companion for my own maid, who is already sulking because the place is so lonely."

MARY LOUISE GROWS SUSPICIOUS 111

And presently Sarah Judd came out upon the lawn to ask Mrs Conant's further instructions and this gave Agatha the desired opportunity to examine her closely. The inspection must have been satisfactory, for an expression of distinct relief crossed the lovely face.

That Sunday evening they all went down to the Bigbee place in Miss Lord's motor car, where the lady entertained her guests at a charming luncheon. The Bigbee place was more extensive than Hillcrest Lodge, as it consisted of a big, rambling residence and numerous outbuildings; but it was not nearly so cosy or homelike, nor so pleasantly situated.

Miss Lord's maid, Susan, was somewhat a mystery to the Hillcrest people. She dressed almost as elaborately as her mistress and performed her duties grudgingly and with a scowl that seemed to resent Miss Lord's entertaining company. Stranger still, when they went home that night it was the maid who brought out the big touring car and drove them all back to Hillcrest Lodge in it, handling the machine as expertly as Agatha could do. Miss Lord pleaded a headache as an excuse for not driving them herself.

Sarah Judd opened the door for them. As she stood under the full light of the hall lamp Mary Louise noticed that the maid Susan leaned from her seat in the car and fixed a shrewd glance on Sarah's unconscious face. Then she gave a little shake of her head and drove away.

"There's something queer about the folks at Bigbee's," Mary Louise confided to Irene, as she went to her friend's room to assist her in preparing for bed. "Agatha Lord kept looking at that velvet ribbon around your neck, tonight, as if she couldn't keep her eyes off it, and this afternoon she seemed scared by the news of Sarah Judd's arrival and wasn't happy until she had seen her. Then, again, that queer maid of Agatha's, Susan, drove us home so she could see Sarah Judd for herself. How do you account for all that, Irene?"

"I don't account for it, my dear. You've been mixed up with so many mysteries that you attach suspicion to the most commonplace events. What should there be about Sarah Judd to frighten anyone?"

"She's a stranger here, that's all, and our neighbors seem suspicious of strangers. I'm not questioning poor, innocent Sarah, understand; but if Agatha and her maid are uneasy about strangers coming here it seems likely there's a reason for it."

"You're getting morbid, Mary Louise. I think I must forbid you to read any more of my romances," said Irene lightly, but at heart she questioned the folks at Bigbee's as seriously as her friend did.

"Don't you think Agatha Lord stole that missing book?" asked Mary Louise, after a little reflection.

"Why should she?" Irene was disturbed by the question but was resolved not to show it.

"To get the letter that was in it—the letter you would not let me read."

"What are your affairs to Agatha Lord?"

"I wish I knew," said Mary Louise, musingly. "Irene, I've an idea she came to Bigbee's just to be near us. There's something stealthy and underhanded about our neighbors, I'm positive. Miss Lord is a very delightful woman, on the surface, but—"

Irene laughed softly, as if amused.

"There can be no reason in the world, Mary Louise," she averred, "why your private affairs are of any interest to outsiders, except—"

"Well, Irene?"

"Except that you are connected, in a way, with your grandfather."

"Exactly! That is my idea, Irene. Ever since that affair with O'Gorman, I've had a feeling that I was being spied upon."

"But that would be useless. You never hear from Colonel Weatherby, except in the most roundabout ways."

"They don't know that; they think I MIGHT hear, and there's no other way to find where he is. Do you think," she added, "that the Secret Service employs female detectives?"

"Perhaps so. There must be occasions when a woman can discover more than a man."

"Then I believe Miss Lord is working for the Secret Service—the enemies of Gran'pa Jim."

"I can't believe it."

"What is on that black ribbon around your neck?"

"A miniature of my mother."

"Oh. Tonight it got above your dress—the ribbon, I mean—and Agatha kept looking at it."

"A good detective wouldn't be caught doing such a clumsy thing, Mary Louise. And, even if detectives were placed here to watch your actions, they wouldn't be interested in spying upon ME, would they?"

"I suppose not."

"I've never even seen your grandfather and so I must be exempt from suspicion. I advise you, my dear, to forget these apprehensions, which must be purely imaginary. If a thousand spies surrounded you, they could do you no harm, nor even trap you into betraying your grandfather, whose present location is a complete mystery to you."

Mary Louise could not help admitting this was true, so she kissed her friend goodnight and went to her own room.

Left alone, Irene put her hand to the ribbon around her neck and drew from her bosom an old-fashioned oval gold locket, as big as any ordinary watch but thinner. She opened the front of the case and kissed her mother's picture, as was her nightly custom. Then she opened the back and drew out a tightly folded wad of paper. This she carefully spread out before her, when it proved to be the old letter she had found in the book.

Once again she read the letter carefully, poring over the words in deep thought.

"This letter," she murmured, "might indeed be of use to the Government, but it is of far more value to Mary Louise and—to her grandfather. I ought not to lose it; nor ought I to allow anyone to read it, at present. Perhaps, if Agatha Lord has noticed the ribbon I wear, it will be best to find a new hiding place for the letter."

She was in bed now, and lay looking around the room with speculative gaze. Beside her stood her wheeled chair, with its cushion of dark Spanish leather. The girl smiled and, reaching for her work-basket, which was on a stand at the head of the bed, she drew out a pair of scissors and cut some of the stitches of the leathern cushion. Then she tucked the letter carefully inside and with a needle and some black linen thread sewed up the place she had ripped open.

She had just completed this task when she glanced up and saw a face at her window—indistinctly, for even as she raised her head it drew back and faded into the outer gloom.

For a moment Irene sat motionless, looking at the window. Then she turned to the stand, where the lamp was, and extinguished the light.

An hour, perhaps, she sat upright in bed, considering what she should do. Then again she reached out in the darkness and felt for her scissors. Securing them, she drew the chair cushion upon the bed and felt along its edge for the place she had sewn. She could not determine for some time which was the right edge but at last she found where the stitches seemed a little tighter drawn than elsewhere and this place she managed to rip open. To her joy she found the letter and drew it out with a sigh of relief.

But now what to do with it was a question of vital importance. She dared not relight her lamp and she was helpless when out of her chair. So she put back the cushion, slid from the bed

MARY LOUISE GROWS SUSPICIOUS

into the chair and wheeled herself in the dark to her dresser, which had a chenille cover. Underneath this cover she spread the letter, deeming that so simple a hiding-place was likely to be overlooked in a hasty search and feeling that the letter would be safe there for the night, at least.

She now returned to her bed. There was no use trying to resew the cushion in the dark. She lay awake for a long time, feeling a certain thrill of delight in the belief that she was a conspirator despite her crippled condition and that she was conspiring for the benefit of her dear friend Mary Louise. Finally she sank into a deep slumber and did not waken till the sun was streaming in at the window and Mary Louise knocked upon her door to call her.

"You're lazy this morning," laughed Mary Louise, entering. "Let me help you dress for breakfast."

Irene thanked her. No one but this girl friend was ever permitted to assist her in dressing, as she felt proud of her ability to serve herself. Her toilet was almost complete when Mary Louise suddenly exclaimed:

"Why, what has become of your chair cushion?"

Irene looked toward the chair. The cushion was gone.

"Never mind," she said, although her face wore a troubled expression. "I must have left it somewhere. Here; I'll put a pillow in its place until I find it."

XIX

AN ARTFUL CONFESSION

This Monday morning Bub appeared at the Lodge and had the car ready before Mr Conant had finished his breakfast. Mary Louise decided to drive to Millbank with them, just for the pleasure of the trip, and although the boy evidently regarded her presence with distinct disapproval he made no verbal objection.

As Irene wheeled herself out upon the porch to see them start, Mary Louise called to her:

"Here's your chair cushion, Irene, lying on the steps and quite wet with dew. I never supposed you could be so careless. And you'd better sew up that rip before it gets bigger," she added, handing the cushion to her friend.

"I will," Irene quietly returned.

Bub proved himself a good driver before they had gone a mile and it pleased Mr Conant to observe that the boy made the trip down the treacherous mountain road with admirable caution. Once on the level, however, he "stepped on it," as he expressed it, and dashed past the Huddle and over the plain as if training for the Grand Prix.

It amused Mary Louise to watch their quaint little driver, barefooted and in blue-jeans and hickory shirt, with the heavy Scotch golf cap pulled over his eyes, taking his task of handling the car as seriously as might any city chauffeur and executing it fully as well.

During the trip the girl conversed with Mr Conant.

"Do you remember our referring to an old letter, the other day?" she asked.

"Yes," said he.

"Irene found it in one of those second-hand books you bought in New York, and she said it spoke of both my mother and my grandfather."

"The deuce it did!" he exclaimed, evidently startled by the information.

"It must have been quite an old letter," continued Mary Louise, musingly.

"What did it say?" he demanded, rather eagerly for the unemotional lawyer.

"I don't know. Irene wouldn't let me read it."

"Wouldn't, eh? That's odd. Why didn't you tell me of this before I left the Lodge?"

"I didn't think to tell you, until now. And, Uncle Peter, what, do you think of Miss Lord?"

"A very charming lady. What did Irene do with the letter?"

"I think she left it in the book; and—the book was stolen the very next day."

"Great Caesar! Who knew about that letter?"

"Miss Lord was present when Irene found the letter, and she heard Irene exclaim that it was all about my mother, as well as about my grandfather."

"Miss Lord?"

"Yes."

"And the book was taken by someone?"

"The next day. We missed it after—after Miss Lord had visited the den alone."

"Huh!"

He rode for awhile in silence.

"Really," he muttered, as if to himself, "I ought to go back. I ought not to take for granted the fact that this old letter is unimportant. However, Irene has read it, and if it happened to be of value I'm sure the girl would have told me about it."

"Yes, she certainly would have told you," agreed Mary Louise. "But she declared that even I would not be interested in reading it."

"That's the only point that perplexes me," said the lawyer. "Just—that—one—point."

"Why?" asked the girl.

But Mr Conant did not explain. He sat bolt upright on his seat, staring at the back of Bub's head, for the rest of the journey. Mary Louise noticed that his fingers constantly fumbled with the locket on his watch chain.

As the lawyer left the car at the station he whispered to Mary Louise:

"Tell Irene that I now know about the letter; and just say to her that I consider her a very cautious girl. Don't say anything more. And don't, for heaven's sake, suspect poor Miss Lord. I'll talk with Irene when I return on Friday."

On their way back Bub maintained an absolute silence until after they had passed the Huddle. Before they started to climb the hill road, however, the boy suddenly slowed up, halted the car and turned deliberately in his seat to face Mary Louise.

"Bein' as how you're a gal," said he, "I ain't got much use fer ye, an' that's a fact. I don't say it's your fault, nor that ye wouldn't 'a' made a pass'ble boy ef ye'd be'n borned thet way. But you're right on one thing, an' don't fergit I told ye so: thet woman at Bigbee's ain't on the square."

"How do you know?" asked Mary Louise, delighted to be taken into Bub's confidence—being a girl.

"The critter's too slick," he explained, raising one bare foot to the cushion beside him and picking a sliver out of his toe. "Her

AN ARTFUL CONFESSION 119

eyes ain't got their shutters raised. Eyes're like winders, but hers ye kain't see through. I don't know nuth'n' 'bout that slick gal at Bigbee's an' I don't want to know nuth'n'. But I heer'd what ye said to the boss, an' what he said to you, an' I guess you're right in sizin' the critter up, an' the boss is wrong."

With this he swung round again and started the car, nor did he utter another word until he ran the machine into the garage.

During Mary Louise's absence Irene had had a strange and startling experience with their beautiful neighbor. The girl had wheeled her chair out upon the bluff to sun herself and read, Mrs Conant being busy in the house, when Agatha Lord strolled up to her with a smile and a pleasant "goodmorning."

"I'm glad to find you alone," said she, seating herself beside the wheeled chair. "I saw Mr Conant and Mary Louise pass the Bigbee place and decided this would be a good opportunity for you and me to have a nice, quiet talk together. So I came over."

Irene's face was a bit disdainful as she remarked:

"I found the cushion this morning."

"What cushion do you refer to?" asked Agatha with a puzzled expression.

Irene frowned.

"We cannot talk frankly together when we are at cross purposes," she complained.

"Very true, my dear; but you seem inclined to speak in riddles."

"Do you deny any knowledge of my chair cushion!"

"I do."

"I must accept your statement, of course. What do you wish to say to me, Miss Lord?"

"I would like to establish a more friendly understanding between us. You are an intelligent girl and cannot fail to realize that I have taken a warm interest in your friend Mary Louise Burrows. I want to know more about her, and about her people, who seem to have cast her off. You are able to give me this information, I am sure, and by doing so you may be instrumental in assisting your friend materially."

It was an odd speech; odd and insincere. Irene studied the woman's face curiously.

"Who are you, Miss Lord?" she inquired.

"Your neighbor."

"Why are you our neighbor?"

"I am glad to be able to explain that—to you, in confidence. I am trying to clear the name of Colonel Weatherby from a grave charge—the charge of high treason."

"In other words, you are trying to discover where he is," retorted Irene impatiently.

"No, my dear; you mistake me. It is not important to my mission, at present, to know where Colonel Weatherby is staying. I am merely seeking relevant information, such information as you are in a position to give me."

"I, Miss Lord?"

"Yes. To be perfectly frank, I want to see the letter which you found in that book."

"Why should you attach any importance to that?"

"I was present, you will remember, when you discovered it. I marked your surprise and perplexity—your fear and uncertainty—as you glanced first at the writing and then at Mary Louise. You determined not to show your friend that letter because it would disturb her, yet you inadvertently admitted, in my hearing, that it referred to the girl's mother and—which is vastly more important—to her grandfather."

"Well; what then, Miss Lord?"

"Colonel Weatherby is a man of mystery. He has been hunted by Government agents for nearly ten years, during which time he has successfully eluded them. If you know anything of the Government service you know it has a thousand eyes, ten thousand ears and a myriad of long arms to seize its malefactors. It has not yet captured Colonel Weatherby."

AN ARTFUL CONFESSION

"Why has he been hunted all these years?"

"He is charged, as I said, with high treason. By persistently evading capture he has tacitly admitted his guilt."

"But he is innocent!" cried Irene indignantly.

Miss Lord seemed surprised, yet not altogether ill-pleased, at the involuntary exclamation.

"Indeed!" she said softly. "Could you prove that statement?"

"I—I think so," stammered the girl, regretting her hasty avowal.

"Then why not do so and by restoring Mary Louise to her grandfather make them both happy?"

Irene sat silent, trapped.

"This is why I have come to you," continued Agatha, very seriously. "I am employed by those whose identity I must not disclose to sift this mystery of Colonel Weatherby to the bottom, if possible, and then to fix the guilt where it belongs. By accident you have come into possession of certain facts that would be important in unravelling the tangle, but through your unfortunate affliction you are helpless to act in your own capacity. You need an ally with more strength and experience than yourself, and I propose you accept me as that ally. Together we may be able to clear the name of James J. Hathaway—who now calls himself Colonel James Weatherby—from all reproach and so restore him to the esteem of his fellow men."

"But we must not do that, even if we could!" cried Irene, quite distressed by the suggestion.

"Why not, my dear?"

The tone was so soft and cat-like that it alarmed Irene instantly. Before answering she took time to reflect. To her dismay she found this woman was gradually drawing from her the very information she had declared she would preserve secret. She knew well that she was no match for Agatha Lord in a trial of wits. Her only recourse must be a stubborn refusal to explain anything more.

"Colonel Weatherby," she said slowly, "has better information than I of the charge against him and his reasons for keeping hidden, yet he steadfastly refuses to proclaim his innocence or to prove he is unjustly accused, which he might very well do if he chose. You say you are working in his interests, and, allowing that, I am satisfied he would bitterly reproach anyone who succeeded in clearing his name by disclosing the truth."

This argument positively amazed Agatha Lord, as it might well amaze anyone who had not read the letter. In spite of her supreme confidence of the moment before, the woman now suddenly realized that this promising interview was destined to end disastrously to her plans.

"I am so obtuse that you will have to explain that statement," she said with assumed carelessness; but Irene was now on guard and replied:

"Then our alliance is dissolved. I do not intend, Miss Lord, to betray such information as I may have stumbled upon unwittingly. You express interest in Mary Louise and her grandfather and say you are anxious to serve them. So am I. Therefore I beg you, in their interests, to abandon any further attempt to penetrate the secret."

Agatha was disconcerted.

"Show me the letter," she urged, as a last resort. "If, on reading it, I find your position is justifiable—you must admit it is now bewildering—I will agree to abandon the investigation altogether."

"I will not show you the letter," declared the girl positively.

The woman studied her face.

"But you will consider this conversation confidential, will you not?"

"Since you request it, yes."

"I do not wish our very pleasant relations, as neighbors, disturbed. I would rather the Conants and Mary Louise did not suspect I am here on any especial mission."

"Very well."

"In truth," continued Agatha, "I am growing fond of you all and this is a real vacation to me, after a period of hard work in the city which racked my nerves. Before long I must return to the old strenuous life, so I wish to make the most of my present opportunities."

"I understand."

No further reference was made to the letter or to Colonel Weatherby. They talked of other things for a while and when Miss Lord went away there seemed to exist—at least upon the surface—the same friendly relations that had formerly prevailed between them.

Irene, reflecting upon the interview, decided that while she had admitted more than was wise she had stopped short of exposing the truth about Colonel Weatherby. The letter was safely hidden, now. She defied even Miss Lord to find it. If she could manage to control her tongue, hereafter, the secret was safe in her possession.

Thoughtfully she wheeled herself back to the den and finding the room deserted she ventured to peep into her novel hiding-place. Yes; the precious letter was still safe. But this time, in her abstraction, she failed to see the face at the window.

XX

DIAMOND CUT DIAMOND

Tuesday afternoon Miss Lord's big touring car stood at the door of Hillcrest Lodge, for Agatha had invited the Conant party to ride with her to Millbank. Irene was tucked into the back seat in a comfortable position and beside her sat Mrs Conant, who was going to make a few purchases at the village store. Mary Louise rode on the front seat with Agatha, who loved to drive her car and understood it perfectly.

When they drove away there was no one left in the house but Sarah Judd, the servant girl, who was washing the lunch dishes. Bub was in the shed-like garage, however, washing and polishing Will Morrison's old car, on which the paint was so cracked and faded that the boy's attempt to improve its appearance was a desperate one.

Sarah, through the kitchen window, watched Bub for a time rather sharply. Then she went out on the bluff and looked down in the valley. Miss Lord's big car was just passing the Huddle on its way up the valley.

Sarah turned and reentered the house. Her meek and diffident expression of countenance had quite disappeared. Her face now wore a look of stern determination and the blue eyes deepened and grew shrewd.

She walked straight to the den and without hesitation approached the farther wall and took from its pegs Will Morrison's fine hunting rifle. In the stock was a hollow chamber for cartridges, for the rifle was of the type known as a "repeater." Sliding back the steel plate that hid this cavity, Sarah drew from it a folded paper of a yellow tint and calmly spread it on the table before her. Then she laid down the rifle, placed a chair at the table and with absorbed attention read the letter from beginning to end — the letter that Irene had found in the book.

It was closely written on both sides the thin sheet — evidently of foreign make — and although the writing was faded it was still clearly legible.

After the first perusal Sarah Judd leaned her elbows on the table and her head on her hands and proceeded to study the epistle still more closely. Then she drew from her pocket a notebook and pencil and with infinite care made a copy of the entire letter, writing it in her book in shorthand. This accomplished, she replaced the letter in the rifle stock and hung the weapon on its pegs again.

Both the window and the glass door of the den faced the backyard. Sarah opened the door and stood there in deep thought, watching Bub at his work. Then she returned to the table and opening a drawer drew out a sheet of blank paper. On this she wrote the following words:

"John Folger, 1601 F. Street, Washington, D. C.

Nothing under sterling over letter bobbing every kernel sad mother making frolic better quick. If England rumples paper Russia admires money.

Sarah Judd."

Each word of this preposterous phrasing she wrote after consulting another book hidden cleverly among the coils of her red hair — a tiny book it — was, filled with curious characters. When the writing was finished the girl seemed well satisfied with her work. After tucking away the book in its former place she went to her room, got her purse and then proceeded to the shed and confronted Bub.

"I want you to drive this car to Millbank, to the telegraph office at the railway station," said Sarah.

Bub gave her a scornful look.

"Ye're crazy," he said and went on with his polishing.

"That needn't worry you," retorted the girl.

"It don't," declared Bub.

"You can drive and you're going to," she continued. "I've got to send this telegram quick, and you've got to take it." She opened her purse and placed two coins on the fender of the car. "There's a dollar to pay for the message, and there's a five-dollar gold-piece to pay you for your trouble."

Bub gave a gasp. He came up beside her and stared at the money. Then he turned to look at Sarah Judd.

"What's up?" he demanded.

"Private business. Don't ask questions; you'd only get lies for answers. Go and earn your money."

"Miss' Conant, she's gone to Millbank herself. Ef she sees me there, I'll git fired. The boss'll fire me himself, anyhow, fer usin' the car when he tol' me not to."

"How much do you get a week!" asked Sarah.

"Four bits."

"That's about two dollars a month. In two months the Conants will move back to the city, and by then you'll have earned four dollars. Why, Bub, it's cheaper for you to take this five-dollar gold-piece and get fired, than to work for two months for four dollars."

Bub scratched his head in perplexity.

"Ye ain't count'n' on the fun o' workin'," he suggested.

"I'm counting on that five dollars—eight bits to a dollar, forty bits altogether. Why, it's a fortune, Bub."

He took out his knife, looked around for a stick to whittle and, finding none, put the knife in his pocket with a sigh.

"I guess Will Morrison wouldn't like it," he decided. "Put up yer money, Sairy."

Sarah withdrew the gold-piece and put a larger one in its place.

"There," she said; "let's make it ten dollars, and save time."

Bub's hesitation vanished, but he asked anxiously:

"Tain't go'n' to do no harm to them gals thet's stoppin' here, is it?"

"It is to do them a good turn that I'm sending this telegram."

"Honor bright?"

"Hope to die, Bub."

"All right; I'm off."

He folded the letter, placed it inside his Scotch cap and stowed the money carefully in his pocket.

"Don't let any of the folks see you if yon can help it," warned Sarah; "and, whatever happens, don't say anything about that telegram to a living soul. Only—see that it's sent."

"I'm wise," answered Bub and a moment later he started the car and rolled away down the road.

Sarah Judd looked after him with a queer smile on her face. Then she went back to her kitchen and resumed her dish-washing. Presently a scarcely audible sound arrested her attention. It seemed to come from the interior of the Lodge.

Sarah avoided making a particle of noise herself as she stole softly through the dining-room and entered the main hallway. One glance showed her that the front door was ajar and the door of the den closed—exactly the reverse of what they should be. She crept forward and with a sudden movement threw open the door of the den.

A woman stood in the center of the room. As the door opened she swung around and pointed a revolver at Sarah. Then for a moment they silently faced one another.

"Ah," said the woman, with an accent of relief, "you're the servant. Go back to your work. Mrs Conant told me to make myself at home here."

"Yes, I know," replied Sarah sarcastically. "She said she was expecting you and told me it wouldn't do any harm to keep an eye on you while you're here. She said Miss Lord was going to get all the family away, so you could make a careful search of the house, you being Miss Lord's maid, Susan—otherwise known as Nan Shelley, from the Washington Bureau."

Susan's hand shook so ridiculously that she lowered the revolver to prevent its dropping from her grasp. Her countenance expressed chagrin, surprise, anger.

"I don't know you," she said harshly. "Who are you?"

"New at the game," replied Sarah Judd, with a shrug. "You don't know me, Nan, but I know you; and I know your record, too. You're as slick as they make 'em, and the one who calls herself Agatha Lord is just an infantile amateur beside you. But go ahead, Nan; don't let me interrupt your work."

The woman sank into a chair.

"You can't be from the home office," she muttered, staring hard at the girl. "They wouldn't dare interfere with my work here."

"No; I'm not from the home office."

"I knew," said Susan, "as soon as I heard the story of your coming, that it was faked. I'd gamble that you never saw Mrs Morrison in your life."

"You'd win," said Sarah, also taking a chair.

"Then who could have sent you here?"

"Figure it out yourself," suggested Sarah.

"I'm trying to. Do you know what we're after?"

"A clew to Hathaway. Incidentally, any other information concerning him that comes your way. That includes the letter."

"Oh. So you know about the letter, do you?" asked Susan.

"To be sure. And I know that's what you're here for now. Don't let me interrupt you. It's a mighty hard job, finding that letter, and the folks'll be back by and by."

"You're right," exclaimed the woman, rising abruptly. "Go back to your work in the kitchen."

"This is my occupation, just now," retorted Sarah, lolling in her chair. "Go ahead with your search, Nan, and I'll tell you when you are 'hot' or 'cold.'"

"You're an impudent little chit," said Nan tartly. "See here," with a sudden change of voice, "let's pool issues. If we can discover anything important in this place, there's reward enough for us all."

"I am not opposing you," protested Sarah Judd, "I'm not a particle interested in whether you trace Hathaway or not. I don't believe you can do it, though, and that letter you're so eager for won't help you a bit. It was written ten years ago."

"That makes it more important," declared the other, "We've two things to accomplish; one is to locate Hathaway, and the other to secure absolute proof of his guilt."

"I thought he was caught doing the job."

"So he was, in a way. But the Department needs more proof."

Sarah Judd smiled unbelievingly. Then she chuckled. Presently she laughed outright, in genuine merriment, as the thought that amused her grew and expanded.

"What fools—" she said, "what perfect fools—we mortals be!"

All this annoyed Nan Shelley exceedingly. The successful woman detective did not relish being jeered at by a mere girl.

"You've read the letter, I suppose, and are now making fun of me for trying to get it? Perhaps you've hidden it yourself— although that isn't likely. Why can't you give me an honest tip? We're both in the same line, it seems, and both trying to earn an honest living. How about that letter? Is it necessary for me to find it?"

"I've read it," admitted Sarah, "and I know where it is. You might perhaps find it, if you hunted long enough, but it isn't worth your while. It wouldn't help in the least to convict

Hathaway and of course it couldn't tell you where he is now hiding."

"Is this straight?"

"True as gospel."

"Then why don't you prove it by showing me the letter?"

"Because I don't belong on your side of the fence. You're working for one organization and I for another. Any little tip I let slip is just for your personal use. Don't bother about that letter."

Susan—or Nan Shelley—sat for a time in thought. Once in a while she would cast a furtive glance around the room and its wall covered with trophies, and then she would turn to Sarah Judd's placid face.

"Where did the boy go?" she asked abruptly.

"What boy?"

"Bub; in the automobile."

"To Millbank."

"What for?"

"To send a telegram."

"Your report?"

"Yes."

"Important?"

"I think it'll bring things to a climax."

"The Hathaway case?"

"You can guess anything, Nan, if you guess long enough."

Nan rose and put the revolver in her pocket. Then she held out her hand frankly to Sarah Judd.

"If you've beaten me in this affair," she said, with no apparent resentment, "you're clever enough to become famous some day. I'm going to take your advice about the letter and if that climax you're predicting arrives on schedule time I'll not be sorry to quit this dreary, dragging case and pick up a more interesting one."

The tone was friendly and frank. Sarah stretched out her hand to meet that of Nan and in a flash a handcuff snapped over her wrist. With a cry she drew back, but a dextrous twist of her opponent's free hand prisoned her other wrist and she at once realized that she was fairly caught.

"Fine!" she cried admiringly, as she looked at her bonds, "What next, Nan?"

But Nan was too busy to talk. She deftly searched the girl's pocket and found the notebook. The shorthand writing caught her eye at once but the characters were unknown to her.

"Cipher, eh?" she muttered.

"A little code of my own invention," said Sarah. "Sometimes I can't make it out myself."

Nan restored the book and examined Sarah Judd's purse.

"They keep you well supplied with funds, it seems."

"Comes handy in emergencies," was the reply.

"Now let's go to your room."

Sarah, handcuffed, led the way. Nan Shelley made a wonderfully rapid search through every article in the maid's room. The lining of her clothes was inspected, her hair-brush tested for a sliding back, the pictures on the wall, the rug and the bed-clothing examined minutely. Yet all this consumed but a brief period of time and resulted in no important discovery.

"Feel better?" asked Sarah cheerfully.

"You know I do. I'm going to remove these handcuffs, now, and then I'm going home. Come and see me, some time when you feel lonesome. I've only that fool Agatha to talk to and I've an idea you and I might interest each other."

As she spoke she unlocked the manacles and dropped them with a slight click into a concealed pocket of her dark skirt.

"I imagine Agatha isn't REAL brilliant," returned Sarah; "but neither am I. When I'm your age, Nan, I hope to be half as clever. Just now you can twist me around your finger."

Nan regarded her seriously.

"I wish I knew what you are up to," she remarked suspiciously. "You can scarcely conceal your joy, my girl, and that proves I've overlooked something. You've puzzled me, youngster as you are, but you must remember that I'm working in the dark while some mysterious gleam of knowledge lights your way. Put us side by side, on the same track, and I wouldn't be afraid of you, Sarah Judd."

"Don't apologize, Nan; it makes me feel ashamed."

Nan's frown, as she looked into the blue eyes, turned to a smile of appreciation. Sarah also smiled, and then she said:

"Let me make you a cup of tea before you go."

"A good idea. We're friends, then?"

"Why not? One friend is worth a thousand enemies and it's absurd to quarrel with one for doing her duty."

"That's what O'Gorman is always saying. Ever hear of O'Gorman?"

"Yes; he's one of the old stand-bys in the secret service department; but they say he's getting old. Slipped a good many cogs lately, I hear."

"He's the Chief's right hand man. O'Gorman used to have this case—the branch of it I'm now working—but he gave it up and recommended the Chief to put me on the job. Said a woman could trail Mary Louise better than any man and with less chance of discovery; and he was right, for I've lived half a block from her in Dorfield and she never saw my face once. But O'Gorman didn't suspect you were coming into the case and the thing's getting altogether too complicated to suit me."

Sarah was brewing the tea and considered an answer unnecessary. The conversation drifted away from the Hathaway case and into less personal channels. When Nan Shelley finally rose to go there was sincere friendliness in Sarah's "goodbye" and the elder woman said in parting:

"You're the right sort, Sarah. If ever you drift into Washington and need work, come to me and I'll get the Chief to take you on. I know he'd be glad to get you."

"Thank you, Nan," said Sarah meekly.

But there was a smile on her freckled face as she watched her recent acquaintance walk down the road, and it lingered there while she returned to her kitchen and finally washed and put away the long neglected lunch dishes.

Bub dashed into the yard and tooted his horn. Sarah went out to him.

"Ye kin call me lucky, ef ye don't mind," he said with a grin. "Sent yer tel'gram, found out the tenner ye guv me were good, an' got back without the folks gett'n' a single blink at me."

"You're some driver, Bub, and you've got a wise head on your shoulders. If you don't talk about this trip, and I don't, no one will ever know, except we two, that the car has been out of the garage."

XXI

BAD NEWS

Peter Conant had told his wife that he wouldn't be at the Lodge this week until Saturday, as business would prevent his coming earlier, yet the Thursday afternoon train brought him to Millbank and Bill Coombs' stage took him to Hillcrest.

"Why, Peter!" exclaimed Aunt Hannah, when she saw him, "what on earth brought you—"

Then she stopped short, for Peter's eyes were staring more roundly than usual and the hand that fumbled at his locket trembled visibly. He stared at Aunt Hannah, he stared at Irene; but most of all he stared at Mary Louise, who seemed to sense from his manner some impending misfortune.

"H-m," said the lawyer, growing red and then paling; "I've bad news."

He chopped the words off abruptly, as if he resented the necessity of uttering them. His eyes, which had been fixed upon the face of Mary Louise, suddenly wavered and sought the floor.

His manner said more than his words. Mary Louise grew white and pressed her hands to her heart, regarding the lawyer with eyes questioning and full of fear. Irene turned a sympathetic gaze upon her friend and Aunt Hannah came closer to the girl and slipped an arm around her waist, as if to help her to endure this unknown trial. And Mary Louise, feeling she could not bear the suspense, asked falteringly:

"Has—Gran'pa Jim—been—"

"No," said Mr Conant. "No, my dear, no."

"Then—has anything happened to—to—mother?"

"Well, well," muttered the lawyer, with a sort or growl, "Mrs Burrows has not been in good health for some months, it seems. She—eh—was under a—eh—under a nervous strain; a severe nervous strain, you know, and—"

"Is she dead?" asked the girl in a low, hard voice.

"The end, it seems, came unexpectedly, several days ago. She did not suffer, your grandfather writes, but—"

Again he left his sentence unfinished, for Mary Louise had buried her face in Aunt Hannah's bosom and was sobbing in a miserable, heart-breaking way that made Peter jerk a handkerchief from, his pocket and blow his nose lustily. Then he turned and marched from the room, while his wife led the hapless girl to a sofa and cuddled her in her lap as if she had been a little child.

"She's best with the women," muttered Peter to himself. "It's a sorrowful thing—a dreadful thing, in a way—but it can't be helped and—she's best with the women."

He had wandered into the dining-room, where Sarah Judd was laying the table for dinner. She must have overheard the conversation in the living room, for she came beside the lawyer and asked:

"When did Mrs Burrows die?"

"On Monday."

"Where?"

"That's none of your business, my girl."

"Has the funeral been held?"

He regarded her curiously. The idea of a servant asking such questions! But there was a look in Sarah's blue eyes that meant more than curiosity; somehow, it drew from him an answer.

"Mrs Burrows was cremated on Wednesday. It seems she preferred it to burial." Having said this, he turned to stare from the window again.

Sarah Judd stood silent a moment. Then she said with a sigh of relief:

"It's a queer world, isn't it, Mr Conant? And this death isn't altogether a calamity."

"Eh? Why not?" whirling round to face her.

"Because," said Sarah, "it will enable Mr Hathaway to face the world again—a free man."

Peter Conant was so startled that he stood motionless, forgetting his locket but not forgetting to stare. Sarah, with her hands full of forks and spoons, began placing the silver in orderly array upon the table. She paid no heed to the lawyer, who gradually recovered his poise and watched her with newly awakened interest. Once or twice he opened his mouth to speak, and then decided not to. He was bewildered, perplexed, suspicious. In thought he began to review the manner of Sarah's coming to them, and her subsequent actions. She seemed a capable servant. Mrs Conant had never complained of her. Yet—what did she know of Hathaway?

Mary Louise did not appear at dinner. She begged to be left alone in her room. Sarah took her some toast and tea, with honest sympathy in her eyes, but the sorrowing girl shook her head and would not taste the food. Later, however, in the evening, she entered the living room where the others sat in depressed silence and said:

"Please, Mr Conant, tell me all you know about—mother."

"It is very little, my dear," replied the lawyer in a kindly tone. "This morning I received a message from your grandfather which said: 'Poor Beatrice passed away on Monday and at her request her body was cremated today. Be very gentle in breaking the sad news to Mary Louise.' That was all, my child, and I came here as quickly as I could. In a day or so we shall have further details, I feel sure. I am going back to town in the morning and will send you any information I receive."

"Thank you," said the girl, and was quietly leaving the room when Irene called to her.

"Mary Louise!"

"Yes?" half turning.

"Will you come with me to my room?"

"Now?"

"Yes. You know I cannot go up the stairs. And—I lost my own dear mother not long ago, you will remember."

Tears started to the girl's eyes, but she waited until Irene wheeled her chair beside her and then the two went through the den to Irene's room.

Mrs Conant nodded to Peter approvingly.

"Irene will comfort her," she said, "and in a way far better than I might do. It is all very dreadful and very sad, Peter, but the poor child has never enjoyed much of her mother's society and when the first bitter grief is passed I think she will recover something of her usual cheerfulness."

"H-m," returned the lawyer; "it seems a hard thing to say, Hannah, but this demise may prove a blessing in disguise and be best for the child's future happiness. In any event, I'm sure it will relieve the strain many of us have been under for the past ten years."

"You talk in riddles, Peter."

"The whole thing is a riddle, Hannah. And, by the way, have you noticed anything suspicious about our hired girl?"

"About Sarah? No," regarding him with surprise.

"Does she—eh—snoop around much?"

"No; she's a very good girl."

"Too good to be true, perhaps," observed Peter, and lapsed into thought. Really, it wouldn't matter now how much Sarah Judd—or anyone else—knew of the Hathaway case. The mystery would solve itself, presently.

XXII

THE FOLKS AT BIGBEE'S

Mr Conant decided to take the Friday morning train back to Dorfield, saying it would not be possible for him to remain at the Lodge over Sunday, because important business might require his presence in town.

"This demise of Mrs Burrows," he said confidentially to his wife in the privacy of their room, "may have far-reaching results and turn the whole current of Colonel Weatherby's life."

"I don't see why," said Aunt Hannah.

"You're not expected to see why," he replied. "As the Colonel is my most important client, I must be at the office in case of developments or a sudden demand for my services. I will tell you one thing, however, and that is that this vacation at Hillcrest Lodge was planned by the Colonel while I was in New York, with the idea that he and Mrs Burrows would come here secretly and enjoy a nice visit with Mary Louise."

"You planned all that, Peter!"

"Yes. That is, Weatherby planned it. He knows Will Morrison well, and Will was only too glad to assist him; so they wired me to come to New York, where all was quickly arranged. This place is so retired that we considered it quite safe for the fugitives to come here."

"Why didn't they come, then?"

"Two reasons prevented them. One was the sudden breaking of Mrs Burrows' health; the other reason was the Colonel's discovery that in some way our carefully laid plans had become known to the detectives who are seeking him."

"Good gracious! Are you sure of that, Peter!"

"The Colonel seemed sure. He maintains a detective force on his own account and his spies discovered that Hillcrest is being watched by agents of the Secret Service."

"Dear me; what a maze of deceit!" wailed the good woman. "I wish you were well out of the whole affair, Peter; and I wish Mary Louise was out of it, too."

"So do I, with all my heart. But it's coming to a focus soon, Hannah. Be patient and it may end better than we now fear."

So Bub drove Mr Conant to Millbank and then the boy took the car to the blacksmith shop to have a small part repaired. The blacksmith made a bungle of it and wasted all the forenoon before he finally took Bub's advice about shaping it and the new rod was attached and found to work successfully.

It was after one o'clock when the boy at last started for home and on the way was hailed by a stranger—a little man who was trudging along the road with both hands thrust in his pockets.

"Going far?" he asked.

"Up th' mount'n to Hillcrest," said Bub.

"Oh. May I have a lift?"

"How fer?"

"Well, I can't say how far I'll go. I'm undecided. Just came out here for a little fresh air, you know, with no definite plans," explained the stranger.

"Hop in," said Bub and for a time they rode together in silence.

"This 'ere's the Huddle, as we're comin' to," announced the boy. "Ol' Miss' Parsons she sometimes takes boarders."

"That's kind of her," remarked the stranger. "But the air isn't so good as further up the hill."

"Ef ye go up," said Bub with a grin, "guess ye'll hev to camp out an' eat scrub. Nobody don't take boarders, up th' mount'n."

"I suppose not."

He made no demand to be let out at the Huddle, so Bub drove on.

"By the way," said the little man, "isn't there a place called Bigbee's, near here?"

"Comin' to it pretty soon. They's some gals livin' there now, so ye won't care to stop."

"What sort of girls are they?"

"Sort o' queer."

"Yes?"

"Ye bet ye. Come from the city a while ago an' livin' by theyselves. Someth'n' wrong 'bout them gals," added Bub reflectively.

"In what way?" asked the little man in a tone of interest.

"They ain't here fer nuth'n' special 'cept watchin' the folks at Hillcrest. Them's the folks I belongs to. For four bits a week. They's someth'n' queer 'bout them, too; but I guess all the folks is queer thet comes here from the city."

"Quite likely," agreed the little man, nodding. "Let me out at Bigbee's, please, and I'll look over those women and form my own opinion of them. They may perhaps be friends of mine."

"In thet case," asserted Bub, "I pity ye, stranger. F'r my part, I ain't got no use fer anything thet wears skirts—'cept one er two, mebbe," he added reflectively. "Most men I kin git 'long with fust-rate; but ef a man ever gits in trouble, er begins cussin' an' acts ugly, it's 'cause some gal's rubbed him crossways the grain er stuck a knife in him an' twisted the blade—so's ter speak."

"You're an observant lad, I see."

"When I'm awake I kain't help seein' things."

"And you're a pastoral philosopher."

Bub scowled and gave him a surly glance.

"What's the use firin' thet high-brow stuff at me?" he asked indignantly. "I s'pose ye think I'm a kid, jes' 'cause I don't do no fancy talkin'."

"I suspect you of nothing but generosity in giving me this ride," said the stranger pleasantly. "Is that Bigbee's, over yonder?"

"Yes."

The little man got out at the point where the Bigbee drive met the road, and walked up the drive toward the house. Agatha Lord was standing at the gateway, as he approached it, and seemed rather startled at his appearance. But she quickly controlled her surprise and asked in a calm voice, as she faced him:

"What's up, O'Gorman?"

"Hathaway's coming here," he said.

"Are you sure?"

"He's in Dorfield today, waiting to see Lawyer Conant, who went in on the morning train. Where's Nan?"

"Here, my lord!" said Nan Shelley, stepping from behind a tall shrub. "How are you, partner? I recognized you as you passed the Huddle with the boy."

"Field glasses, eh? There isn't much escapes you, Nan."

"Why didn't you tell me?" asked Agatha reproachfully.

"Why don't you make your own discoveries?" retorted her confederate. Then, turning to O'Gorman, she continued: "So Hathaway's coming, is he? At last."

"A little late, but according to program. How have you been getting along?"

"Bored to death," asserted Nan. "Agatha has played the lady and I've done the dirty work. But tell me, why didn't you nab Hathaway at Dorfield?"

O'Gorman smiled a little grimly as he answered:

"I'm not sure, Nan, that we shall nab Hathaway at all."

"Isn't he being shadowed?" with some surprise.

"No. But he'll come here, right enough; and then—"

"And then," she added, as he paused, "the chase of years will come to an end."

"Exactly. We may decide to take him to Washington, and we may not."

She gazed at him inquiringly.

"There are some new developments, then, O'Gorman?"

"I'm inclined to suspect there are."

"Known to the department?"

"Yes. I'm to investigate and use my judgment."

"I see. Then Agatha and I are out of it?"

"Not yet; I'm still depending on your shrewdness to assist me. The office has only had a hint, so far, of the prospective break in the case, but—"

"Oh, yes; I remember now," exclaimed Nan.

"That girl up at Conant's sent a telegram, in a desperate hurry. I suspected it meant something important. Who is she, O'Gorman, and why did the Chief cut under us by planting Sarah Judd in the Conants' household?"

"He didn't. The girl has nothing to do with the Department."

"Then some of you intercepted the telegram?"

"We know what it said," he admitted. "Come, let's go to the house. I've had no lunch. Can you feed me?"

"Certainly." They turned and walked slowly up the path. Said Nan, musingly: "That Sarah Judd is rather clever, O'Gorman. Is she in Hathaway's pay?"

"I think not," he replied, with an amused chuckle.

Nan tossed her head indignantly.

"Very well; play me for a ninny, if you like," she said resentfully. "You'll get a heap more out of me, in that way!"

"Now, now," said Agatha warningly, "keep your tempers and don't quarrel. You two are like cats and dogs when you get together; yet you're the two cleverest people in the service. According to your story, Mr O'Gorman, there's an important crisis approaching, and we'd all like to be able to render a good account of ourselves."

Agatha Lord may have lacked something of Nan's experience, but this speech proved her a fair diplomat. It dispersed the gathering storm and during the rest of that afternoon the three counseled together in perfect harmony, O'Gorman confiding to his associates such information as would enable them to act with him intelligently. Hathaway and Peter Conant could not arrive till the next day at noon; they might even come by the afternoon train. Nan's field glasses would warn them of the arrival and meanwhile there was ample time to consider how they should act.

XXIII

A KISS FROM JOSIE

That evening, as Sarah Judd was sitting in her room reading a book, her work for the day being over, she heard a succession of little taps against her window-pane. She sat still, listening, until the taps were repeated, when she walked straight to the window, drew the shade and threw tip the sash. O'Gorman's face appeared in the opening and the girl put a hand on each of his cheeks and leaning over kissed him full upon his lips.

The man's face, lighted by the lamp from within the room, was radiant. Even the fat nose was beatified by the love that shone in his small gray eyes. He took one of her hands in both of his own and held it close a moment, while they regarded one another silently.

Then he gave a little beckoning signal and the girl turned to slip on a light coat, for the nights were chill on the mountain. Afterward she unfastened her outside door and joined the detective, who passed an arm around her and led her to one of the benches on the bluff.

The new moon was dim, but a sprinkling of stars lit the sky. The man and girl were far enough from the Lodge not to be overheard.

"It's good to see you again, Josie," said O'Gorman, as they seated themselves on the bench. "How do you like being a sleuth?"

"Really, Daddy," she replied, "it has been no end of a lark. I'm dead sick of washing other folks' dishes, I confess, but the fun I've had has more than made up for the hard work. Do you know, Dad, I had a session with Nan Shelley one day, and she didn't have much the best of it, either, although she's quick as a cat and had me backed off the map in every way except for the matter of wits. My thoughts didn't crumble much and Nan was good enough to congratulate me. She knew, as soon as I did, about the letter the crippled girl found in a book, but I managed to make a copy of it, while Nan is still wondering where it is hid. I'm patting myself on the back, Dad, because you trained me and I want to prove myself a credit to your training. It's no wonder, with such a master, that I could hold my own with Nan Shelley!"

He gave a little amused laugh.

"You're all right, Josie dear," he replied. "My training wouldn't have amounted to shucks if you hadn't possessed the proper gray matter to work with. But about that letter," more seriously; "your telegram told me a lot, because our code is so concise, but it also left a good deal to be guessed at. Who wrote the letter? I must know all the details in order to understand it properly."

"It's all down in my private shorthand book," said Josie O'Gorman, "but I've never dared make a clear copy while Nan was so near me. You can't read it, Dad, and I can't read it to you in the dark; so you'll have to wait."

"Have you your notebook here?"

"Always carry it."

He drew an electric storage-lamp from his pocket and shielded the tiny circle of light with his coat.

"Now, then," said he, "read the letter to me, Josie. It's impossible for anyone to see the light from the house."

The girl held her notebook behind the flap of his coat, where the lamp shed its white rays upon it, and slowly read the text of the letter. O'Gorman sat silent for some time after she had finished reading.

"In all my speculations concerning the Hathaway case," he said to his daughter, "I never guessed this as the true solution of the man's extraordinary actions. But now, realizing that Hathaway is a gentleman to the core, I understand he could not have acted in any other way."

"Mrs Burrows is dead," remarked Josie.

"I know. It's a pity she didn't die long ago."

"This thing killed her, Dad."

"I'm sure of it. She was a weak, though kind-hearted, woman and this trouble wore her out with fear and anxiety. How did the girl—Mary Louise—take her mother's death?"

"Rather hard, at first. She's quieter now. But—see here, Dad—are you still working for the Department?"

"Of course."

"Then I'm sorry I've told you so much. I'm on the other side. I'm here to protect Mary Louise Burrows and her interests."

"To be sure. I sent you here myself, at my own expense, both to test your training before I let you into the regular game and for the sake of the little Burrows girl, whom I fell in love with when she was so friendless. I believed things would reach a climax in the Hathaway case, in this very spot, but I couldn't foresee that your cleverness would ferret out that letter, which the girl Irene intended to keep silent about, nor did I know that the Chief would send me here in person to supervise Hathaway's capture. Mighty queer things happen in this profession of ours, and circumstances lead the best of us by the nose."

"Do you intend to arrest Mr Hathaway?"

"After hearing that letter read and in view of the fact that Mrs Burrows is dead, I think not. The letter, if authentic, clears up the mystery to our complete satisfaction. But I must get the story from Hathaway's own lips, and then compare his statement with that in the letter. If they agree, we won't prosecute the man at all, and the famous case that has caused us so much trouble for years will be filed in the office pigeonholes and pass into ancient history."

Josie O'Gorman sat silent for a long time. Then she asked:

"Do you think Mr Hathaway will come here, now that—now that—"

"I'm quite sure he will come."

"When?"

"Tomorrow."

"Then I must warn them and try to head him off. I'm on his side, Dad; don't forget that."

"I won't; and because you're on his side, Josie, you must let him come and be vindicated, and so clear up this matter for good and all."

"Poor Mary Louise! I was thinking of her, not of her grandfather. Have you considered how a knowledge of the truth will affect her?"

"Yes. She will be the chief sufferer when her grandfather's innocence is finally proved."

"It will break her heart," said Josie, with a sigh.

"Perhaps not. She's mighty fond of her grandfather. She'll be glad to have him freed from suspicion and she'll be sorry—about the other thing."

Sarah Judd—otherwise Josie O'Gorman—sighed again; but presently she gave a little chuckle of glee.

"Won't Nan be wild, though, when she finds I've beaten her and won the case for Hathaway?"

"Nan won't mind. She's an old hand at the game and has learned to take things as they come. She'll be at work upon some other case within a week and will have forgotten that this one ever bothered her."

"Who is Agatha Lord, and why did they send her here as principal, with Nan as her maid?"

"Agatha is an educated woman who has moved in good society. The Chief thought she would be more likely to gain the friendship of the Conants than Nan, for poor Nan hasn't much breeding to boast of. But she was really the principal, for all that, and Agatha was instructed to report to her and to take her orders."

"They were both suspicious of me," said the girl, "but as neither of them had ever set eyes on me before I was able to puzzle them. On the other hand, I knew who Nan was because I'd seen her with you, which gave me an advantage. Now, tell me, how's mother?"

"Pretty chirky, but anxious about you because this is your first case and she feared your judgment wasn't sufficiently matured. I told her you'd pull through all right."

For an hour they sat talking together. Then Officer O'Gorman kissed his daughter goodnight and walked back to the Bigbee house.

XXIV

FACING THE TRUTH

Irene was a great comfort to Mary Louise in this hour of trial. The chair-girl, beneath her gaiety of demeanor and lightness of speech, was deeply religious. Her absolute faith sounded so cheering that death was robbed of much of its horror and her bereaved friend found solace. Mary Louise was able to talk freely of "Mamma Bee" to Irene, while with Aunt Hannah she rather avoided reference to her mother.

"I've always longed to be more with Mamma Bee and to learn to know her better," she said to her friend; "for, though she was very loving and gentle to me while I was with her, she spent most of her life caring for Gran'pa Jim, and they were away from me so much that I really didn't get to know Mamma very well. I think she worried a good deal over Gran'pa's troubles. She couldn't help that, of course, but I always hoped that some day the troubles would be over and we could all live happily together. And now—that can never be!"

Irene, knowing more of the Hathaway family history than Mary Louise did, through the letter she had found and read, was often perplexed how to console her friend and still regard honesty and truth. Any deception, even when practiced through the best of motives, was abhorrent to her nature, so she avoided speaking of the present affliction and led Mary Louise to look to a future life for the motherly companionship she had missed on earth.

"That," said she, "is the thought that has always given me the most comfort. We are both orphans, dear, and I'm sure your nature is as brave as my own and that you can bear equally well the loss of your parents."

And Mary Louise was really brave and tried hard to bear her grief with patient resignation. One thing she presently decided in her mind, although she did not mention it to Irene. She must find Gran'pa Jim and go to him, wherever he might be. Gran'pa Jim and her mother had been inseparable companions; Mary Louise knew that her own present sorrow could be nothing when compared with that of her grandfather. And so it was her duty to find him and comfort him, to devote her whole life, as her mother had done, to caring for his wants and cheering his loneliness—so far, indeed, as she was able to do. Of course, no one could quite take the place of Mamma Bee.

She was thinking in this vein as she sat in the den with Irene that Saturday afternoon. The chair-girl, who sewed beautifully, was fixing over one of Mary Louise's black dresses while Mary Louise sat opposite, listlessly watching her. The door into the hall was closed, but the glass door to the rear porch was wide open to let in the sun and air. And this simple scene was the setting for the drama about to be enacted.

Mary Louise had her back half turned to the hall door, which Irene partially faced, and so it was that when the door opened softly and the chair-girl raised her head to gaze with startled surprise at someone who stood in the doorway, Mary Louise first curiously eyed her friend's expressive face and then, rather languidly, turned her head to glance over her shoulder.

The next moment she sprang to her feet and rushed forward.

"Gran'pa Jim—Oh, Gran'pa Jim!" she cried, and threw herself into the arms of a tall man who folded her to his breast in a close embrace.

FACING THE TRUTH

For a while they stood there silent, while Irene dropped her eyes to her lap, deeming the reunion too sacred to be observed by another. And then a little stir at the open porch door attracted her attention and with a shock of repulsion she saw Agatha Lord standing there with a cynical smile on her lovely face. Softly the sash of the window was raised, and the maid Susan stood on the ground outside, leaned her elbows on the sill and quietly regarded the scene within the den.

The opening of the window arrested Colonel Weatherby's attention. He lifted his head and with a quick glance took in the situation. Then, still holding his granddaughter in his arms, he advanced to the center of the room and said sternly, addressing Agatha:

"Is this a deliberate intrusion, because I am here, or is it pure insolence?"

"Forgive us if we intrude, Mr Hathaway," replied Agatha. "It was not our desire to interrupt your meeting with your granddaughter, but—it has been so difficult, in the past, to secure an interview with you, sir, that we dared not risk missing you at this time."

He regarded her with an expression of astonishment.

"That's it, exactly, Mr Weatherby-Hathaway," remarked Susan mockingly, from her window.

"Don't pay any attention to them, Gran'pa Jim," begged Mary Louise, clinging to him. "They're just two dreadful women who live down below here, and—and—"

"I realize who they are," said the old gentleman in a calm voice, and addressing Agatha again he continued: "Since you are determined to interview me, pray step inside and be seated."

Agatha shook her head with a smile; Nan Shelley laughed outright and retorted:

"Not yet, Hathaway. We can't afford to take chances with one who has dodged the whole Department for ten years."

"Then you are Government agents?" he asked.

"That's it, sir."

He turned his head toward the door by which he had entered, for there was an altercation going on in the hallway and Mr Conant's voice could be heard angrily protesting.

A moment later the lawyer came in, followed by the little man with the fat nose, who bowed to Colonel Weatherby very respectfully yet remained planted in the doorway.

"This is—er—er—very unfortunate, sir; ve-ry un-for-tu-nate!" exclaimed Peter Conant, chopping off each word with a sort of snarl. "These con-found-ed secret service people have trailed us here."

"It doesn't matter, Mr Conant," replied the Colonel, in a voice composed but very weary. He seated himself in a chair, as he spoke, and Mary Louise sat on the arm of it, still embracing him.

"No," said O'Gorman, "it really doesn't matter, sir. In fact, I'm sure you will feel relieved to have this affair off your mind and be spared all further annoyance concerning it."

The old gentleman looked at him steadily but made no answer. It was Peter Conant who faced the speaker and demanded:

"What do you mean by that statement?"

"Mr Hathaway knows what I mean. He can, in a few words, explain why he has for years borne the accusation of a crime of which he is innocent."

Peter Conant was so astounded he could do nothing but stare at the detective. Staring was the very best thing that Peter did and he never stared harder in his life. The tears had been coursing down Mary Louise's cheeks, but now a glad look crossed her face.

"Do you hear that, Gran'pa Jim?" she cried. "Of course you are innocent! I've always known that; but now even your enemies do."

Mr Hathaway looked long into the girl's eyes, which met his own hopefully, almost joyfully. Then he turned to O'Gorman.

"I cannot prove my innocence," he said.

"Do you mean that you WILL not?"

"I will go with you and stand my trial. I will accept whatever punishment the law decrees."

O'Gorman nodded his head.

"I know exactly how you feel about it, Mr Hathaway," he said, "and I sympathize with you most earnestly. Will you allow me to sit down awhile? Thank you."

He took a chair facing that of the hunted man. Agatha, seeing this, seated herself on the door-step. Nan maintained her position, leaning through the open window.

"This," said O'Gorman, "is a strange case. It has always been a strange case, sir, from the very beginning. Important government secrets of the United States were stolen and turned over to the agent of a foreign government which is none too friendly to our own. It was considered, in its day, one of the most traitorous crimes in our history. And you, sir, a citizen of high standing and repute, were detected in the act of transferring many of these important papers to a spy, thus periling the safety of the nation. You were caught red-handed, so to speak, but made your escape and in a manner remarkable and even wonderful for its adroitness have for years evaded every effort on the part of our Secret Service Department to effect your capture. And yet, despite the absolute truth of this statement, you are innocent."

None cared to reply for a time. Some who had listened to O'Gorman were too startled to speak; others refrained. Mary Louise stared at the detective with almost Peter Conant's expression—her eyes big and round. Irene thrilled with joyous anticipation, for in the presence of this sorrowing, hunted, white-haired old man, whose years had been devoted to patient self-sacrifice, the humiliation the coming disclosure would, thrust upon Mary Louise seemed now insignificant. Until this moment Irene had been determined to suppress the knowledge gained through the old letter in order to protect the feelings of her friend, but now a crying need for the truth to prevail was borne in upon her. She had thought that she alone knew this truth. To her astonishment, as well as satisfaction, the chair-girl now discovered that O'Gorman was equally well informed.

XXV

SIMPLE JUSTICE

All eyes were turned upon Mr Hathaway, who had laid a hand upon the head of his grandchild and was softly stroking her hair. At last he said brokenly, repeating his former assertion:

"I cannot prove my innocence."

"But I can," declared O'Gorman positively, "and I'm going to do it."

"No—no!" said Hathaway, startled at his tone.

"It's this way, sir," explained the little man in a matter-of-fact voice, "this chase after you has cost the government a heavy sum already, and your prosecution is likely to make public an affair which, under the circumstances, we consider it more diplomatic to hush up. Any danger to our country has passed, for information obtained ten years ago regarding our defenses, codes, and the like, is today worthless because all conditions are completely changed. Only the crime of treason remains; a crime that deserves the severest punishment; but the guilty persons have escaped punishment and are now facing a higher tribunal—both the principal in the crime and his weak and foolish tool. So it is best for all concerned, Mr Hathaway, that we get at the truth of this matter and, when it is clearly on record in the government files, declare the case closed for all time. The State Department has more important matters that demand its attention."

The old man's head was bowed, his chin resting on his breast. It was now the turn of Mary Louise to smooth his thin gray locks.

"If you will make a statement, sir," continued O'Gorman, "we shall be able to verify it."

Slowly Hathaway raised his head.

"I have no statement to make," he persisted.

"This is rank folly," exclaimed O'Gorman, "but if you refuse to make the statement, I shall make it myself."

"I beg you — I implore you!" said Hathaway pleadingly.

The detective rose and stood before him, looking not at the old man but at the young girl — Mary Louise.

"Tell me, my child," he said gently, "would you not rather see your grandfather — an honorable, high-minded gentleman — acquitted of an unjust accusation, even at the expense of some abasement and perhaps heart-aches on your part, rather than allow him to continue to suffer disgrace in order to shield you from so slight an affliction?"

"Sir!" cried Hathaway indignantly, starting to his feet; "how dare you throw the burden on this poor child? Have you no mercy — no compassion?"

"Plenty," was the quiet reply. "Sit down, sir. This girl is stronger than you think. She will not be made permanently unhappy by knowing the truth, I assure you."

Hathaway regarded him with a look of anguish akin to fear. Then he turned and seated himself, again putting an arm around Mary Louise as if to shield her.

Said Irene, speaking very slowly:

"I am quite sure Mr O'Gorman is right. Mary Louise is a brave girl, and she loves her grandfather."

Then Mary Louise spoke — hesitatingly, at first, for she could not yet comprehend the full import of the officer's words.

"If you mean," said she, "that it will cause me sorrow and humiliation to free my grandfather from suspicion, and that he refuses to speak because he fears the truth will hurt me, then I ask you to speak out, Mr O'Gorman."

"Of course," returned the little man, smiling at her approvingly; "that is just what I intend to do. All these years, my girl, your grandfather has accepted reproach and disgrace in order to shield the good name of a woman and to save her from a prison cell. And that woman was your mother."

"Oh!" cried Mary Louise and covered her face with her hands.

"You brute!" exclaimed Hathaway, highly incensed.

"But this is not all," continued O'Gorman, unmoved; "your mother, Mary Louise, would have been condemned and imprisoned—and deservedly so in the eyes of the law—had the truth been known; and yet I assure you she was only guilty of folly and of ignorance of the terrible consequences that might have resulted from her act. She was weak enough to be loyal to a promise wrung from her in extremity, and therein lay her only fault. Your grandfather knew all this, and she was his daughter—his only child. When the accusation for your mother's crime fell on him, he ran away and so tacitly admitted his guilt, thus drawing suspicion from her. His reason for remaining hidden was that, had he been caught and brought to trial, he could not have lied or perjured himself under oath even to save his dearly loved daughter from punishment. Now you understand why he could not submit to arrest; why, assisted by a small but powerful band of faithful friends, he has been able to evade capture during all these years. I admire him for that; but he has sacrificed himself long enough. Your mother's recent death renders her prosecution impossible. It is time the truth prevailed. In simple justice I will not allow this old man to embitter further his life, just to protect his grandchild from a knowledge of her mother's sin."

Again a deathly silence pervaded the room.

"You—you are speaking at random," said Hathaway, in a voice choked with emotion. "You have no proof of these dreadful statements."

"But *I* have!" said Irene bravely, believing it her duty to support O'Gorman.

"And so have I," asserted the quiet voice of Sarah Judd, who had entered the room unperceived.

Hathaway regarded both the girls in surprise, but said nothing.

"I think," said Officer O'Gorman, "it will be best for us to read to Mr Hathaway that letter."

"The letter which I found in the book?" asked Irene eagerly.

"Yes. But do not disturb yourself," as she started to wheel her chair close to the wall. "Josie will get it."

To Irene's astonishment Sarah Judd walked straight to the repeating rifle, opened the sliding plate in its stock and took out the closely folded letter. Perhaps Nan Shelley and Agatha Lord were no less surprised than Irene; also they were deeply chagrined. But O'Gorman's slip in calling Sarah Judd "Josie" had conveyed to his associates information that somewhat modified their astonishment at the girl's cleverness, for everyone who knew O'Gorman had often heard of his daughter Josie, of whom he was accustomed to speak with infinite pride. He always said he was training her to follow his own profession and that when the education was complete Josie O'Gorman would make a name for herself in the detective service. So Nan and Agatha exchanged meaning glances and regarded the freckled-faced girl with new interest.

"I'm not much of a reader," said Josie, carefully unfolding the paper. "Suppose we let Miss Irene read it?"

Her father nodded assent and Josie handed the sheet to Irene.

SIMPLE JUSTICE

Mr Hathaway had been growing uneasy and now addressed Officer O'Gorman in a protesting voice:

"Is this reading necessary, sir?"

"Very necessary, Mr Hathaway."

"What letter is this that you have referred to?"

"A bit of information dating nearly ten years ago and written by one who perhaps knew more of the political intrigues of John and Beatrice Burrows than has ever come to your own knowledge."

"The letter is authentic, then?"

"Quite so."

"And your Department knows of its existence?"

"I am acting under the Department's instructions, sir. Oblige us, Miss Macfarlane," he added, turning to Irene, "by reading the letter in full."

XXVI

THE LETTER

"This sheet," explained Irene, "is, in fact, but a part of a letter. The first sheets are missing, so we don't know who it was addressed to; but it is signed, at the end, by the initials 'E. de V.'"

"The ambassador!" cried Hathaway, caught off his guard by surprise.

"The same," said O'Gorman triumphantly; "and it is all in his well-known handwriting. Read the letter, my girl."

"The first sentence," said Irene, "is a continuation of something on a previous page, but I will read it just as it appears here."

And then, in a clear, distinct voice that was audible to all present, she read as follows:

"which forces me to abandon at once my post and your delightful country in order to avoid further complications. My greatest regret is in leaving Mrs Burrows in so unfortunate a predicament. The lady was absolutely loyal to us and the calamity that has overtaken her is through no fault of her own.

"That you may understand this thoroughly I will remind you that John Burrows was in our employ. It was through our secret influence that he obtained his first government position, where he inspired confidence and became trusted implicitly.

He did not acquire full control, however, until five years later, and during that time he met and married Beatrice Hathaway, the charming daughter of James J. Hathaway, a wealthy broker. That gave Burrows added importance and he was promoted to the high government position he occupied at the time of his death.

"Burrows made for us secret copies of the fortifications on both the east and west coasts, including the number and caliber of guns, amounts of munitions stored and other details. Also he obtained copies of the secret telegraph and naval codes and the complete armaments of all war vessels, both in service and in process of construction. A part of this information and some of the plans he delivered to me before he died, as you know, and he had the balance practically ready for delivery when he was taken with pneumonia and unfortunately expired very suddenly.

"It was characteristic of the man's faithfulness that on his death bed he made his wife promise to deliver the balance of the plans and an important book of codes to us as early as she could find an opportunity to do so. Mrs Burrows had previously been in her husband's confidence and knew he was employed by us while holding his position with the government, so she readily promised to carry out his wishes, perhaps never dreaming of the difficulties that would confront her or the personal danger she assumed. But she was faithful to her promise and afterward tried to fulfill it.

"Her father, the James J. Hathaway above mentioned, in whose mansion Mrs Burrows lived with her only child, is a staunch patriot. Had he known of our plot he would have promptly denounced it, even sacrificing his son-in-law. I have no quarrel with him for that, you may well believe, as I value patriotism above all other personal qualities. But after the death of John Burrows it became very difficult for his wife to find a way to deliver to me the packet of plans without being detected. Through some oversight at the government office, which aroused suspicion immediately after his death, Burrows was discovered to have made duplicates of many documents intrusted to him and with a suspicion of the truth government agents were sent to interview Mrs Burrows and find out if the duplicates were still among her husband's papers. Being a clever woman, she succeeded in secreting the precious package and so foiled the detectives. Even her own father, who was very indignant that a member of his household should be accused of treason, had no suspicion that his daughter was in any way involved. But the house was watched, after that, and Mrs Burrows was constantly under surveillance—a fact of which she was fully aware. I also became aware of the difficulties that surrounded her and although impatient to receive the package I dared not press its delivery. Fortunately no suspicion attached to me and a year or so after her husband's death I met Mrs Burrows at the house of a mutual friend, on the occasion of a crowded reception, and secured an interview with her where we could not be overheard. We both believed that by this time the police espionage had been greatly relaxed so I suggested that she boldly send the parcel to me, under an assumed name, at Carver's Drug Store, where I had a confederate. An ordinary messenger would not do for this errand, but Mr Hathaway drove past the drug store every morning on his way to his office, and Mrs Burrows thought it would be quite safe to send the parcel by his hand, the man being wholly above suspicion.

"On the morning we had agreed upon for the attempt, the woman brought the innocent looking package to her father, as he was leaving the house, and asked him to deliver it at the drug store on his way down. Thinking it was returned goods he consented, but at the moment he delivered the parcel a couple of detectives appeared and arrested him, opening the package before him to prove its important contents. I witnessed this disaster to our plot with my own eyes, but managed to escape without being arrested as a partner in the conspiracy, and thus I succeeded in protecting the good name of my beloved country, which must never be known in this connection.

"Hathaway was absolutely stupefied at the charge against him. Becoming violently indignant, he knocked down the officers and escaped with the contents of the package. He then returned home and demanded an explanation from his daughter, who confessed all.

"It was then that Hathaway showed the stuff he was made of, to use an Americanism. He insisted on shielding his daughter, to whom he was devotedly attached, and in taking all the responsibility on his own shoulders. The penalty of this crime is imprisonment for life and he would not allow Mrs Burrows to endure it. Being again arrested he did not deny his guilt but cheerfully suffered imprisonment. Before the day set for his trial, however, he managed to escape and since then he has so cleverly hidden himself that the authorities remain ignorant of his whereabouts. His wife and his grandchild also disappeared and it was found that his vast business interests had been legally transferred to some of his most intimate friends—doubtless for his future benefit.

"The government secret service was helpless. No one save I knew that Hathaway was shielding his daughter, whose promise to her dead husband had led her to betray her country to the representative of a foreign power such as our own. Yet Hathaway, even in sacrificing his name and reputation, revolted at suffering life-long imprisonment, nor dared he stand trial through danger of being forced to confess the truth. So he remains in hiding and I have hopes that he will be able—through his many influential friends—to save himself from capture for many months to come.

"This is the truth of the matter, dear friend, and as this explanation must never get beyond your own knowledge

I charge you to destroy this letter as soon as it is read. When you are abroad next year we will meet and consider this and other matters in which we are mutually interested. I would not have ventured to put this on paper were it not for my desire to leave someone in this country posted on the Hathaway case. You will understand from the foregoing that the situation has become too delicate for me to remain here. If you can, give aid to Hathaway, whom I greatly admire, for we are in a way responsible for his troubles. As for Mrs Burrows, I consider her a woman of character and honor. That she might keep a pledge made to her dead husband she sinned against the law without realizing the enormity of her offense. If anyone is to blame it is poor John Burrows, who was not justified in demanding so dangerous a pledge from his wife; but he was dying at the time and his judgment was impaired. Let us be just to all and so remain just to ourselves.

"Write me at the old address and believe me to be yours most faithfully

E. de V.

The 16th of September, 1905."

During Irene's reading the others maintained an intense silence. Even when she had ended, the silence continued for a time, while all considered with various feelings the remarkable statement they had just heard.

It was O'Gorman who first spoke.

"If you will assert, Mr Hathaway, that the ambassador's statement is correct, to the best of your knowledge and belief, I have the authority of our department to promise that the charge against you will promptly be dropped and withdrawn and that you will be adjudged innocent of any offense against the law. It is true that you assisted a guilty person to escape punishment, and are therefore liable for what is called 'misprision of treason,' but we shall not press that, for, as I said before, we prefer, since no real harm has resulted, to allow the case to be filed without further publicity. Do you admit the truth of the statements contained in this letter?"

"I believe them to be true," said Mr Hathaway, in a low voice. Mary Louise was nestling close in his arms and now she raised her head tenderly to kiss his cheek. She was not sobbing; she did not even appear to be humbled or heart-broken. Perhaps she did not realize at the moment how gravely her father and mother had sinned against the laws of their country. That realization might come to her later, but just now she was happy in the vindication of Gran'pa Jim—a triumph that overshadowed all else.

"I'll take this letter for our files," said Officer O'Gorman, folding it carefully before placing it in his pocketbook. "And now, sir, I hope you will permit me to congratulate you and to wish you many years of happiness with your granddaughter, who first won my admiration by her steadfast faith in your innocence. She's a good girl, is Mary Louise, and almost as clever as my Josie here. Come, Nan; come, Agatha; let's go back to Bigbee's. Our business here is finished."

> Assembling the greatest detectives all together

Covering the full range and history of detective fiction.
From Zadig, *The Moonstone*, and Dupin through Sherlock Holmes, Loveday Brooke, Montague Egg, Lord Peter Wimsey, *The Thinking Machine*, Father Brown down to Solar Pons.

For more details and a full list of titles:
visit https://www.hachetteindia.com/home/yellowbacks

WELCOME BACK TO THE GOLDEN AGE